I0647898

GULITH
New York

When the Birds Fly South
Stanton A. Coblentz

ISBN: 978-1-63652-326-2

WHEN THE BIRDS FLY SOUTH

STANTON A. COBLENTZ

TABLE OF CONTENTS

I. DRIFTING LEAVES

II. BLOSSOM AND SEED

III. THE WILL OF YULADA

I
DRIFTING LEAVES

CHAPTER I
THE MOUNTAIN OF VANISHED MEN

High among the snow-tipped ranges of Afghanistan, there is a peak notable for its peculiar rocky crown. Unlike its lordly neighbors, it is dominated not by crags and glaciers, but by a projection which seems almost to bear the impress of human hands. From the southern valley, five thousand feet beneath, the traveler will observe a gigantic steel-gray figure carved in the image of a woman; and he will notice that the woman's hands are uplifted in an attitude of prayer, and that she stands with one foot slanted behind her and one foot slightly upraised, as though prepared to step into the abyss. How this lifelike form came to be perched on that desolate eminence is a mystery to the observer; but he assumes that it is a product of some prank of nature, for it is far too large to have been made by man. Yet he must be unimaginative indeed not to be awe-stricken at thought of the forces which gave that colossus birth.

I, for one, shall never forget my first glimpse of the stone Titan. As a member of an American geological expedition studying the mountain strata of Northern India, Afghanistan and Tibet, I had been tramping for hours through a winding rock-defile in company with nine scientific colleagues and the native guides. Suddenly, coming out through a break in the canyon, I looked down into a deep basin densely mantled in deodar and pine. Beyond this valley, to the north, a succession of jagged peaks shot skyward, their lower slopes dark-green with foliage, their upper altitudes bare and brown, and streaked here and there with white. Almost precisely in their center, as though in the acknowledged place of honor, one summit loomed slightly higher and less precipitous than the others, and on its tip the singular statue-like image.

My first impression was that it was an illusion. Never had I or any of my companions heard of such a figure; we were hardly less startled than if we had journeyed to the North Pole, there to gaze at a skyscraper. Eagerly we questioned our Afghan guides, but at first their stolid, swarthy faces simulated indifference, though they cast furtive and even frightened glances at one another. Then, pressed to speak, they assured us that the stone image was the work of devils; and finally they stated that the figure had been created by the "Ibandru," a race of mountain folk with wings like birds and the power of making themselves invisible.

Naturally, my friends and I laughed at such a naïve superstition. Yet when I proposed that we climb the mountain and seek the home of the "Ibandru," our guides repeated their warning that these people were powerful and evil-minded enchanters. And when, not to be daunted by fairy tales, I insisted on investigating the mountain top, the natives betrayed their alarm by their rolling dark eyes and eloquent gestures, and swore that if we ever began the climb we should be unable to return. Scores of their countrymen had been bewitched and lost in seeking the peak, which was known as "The Mountain of Vanished Men"; and for their own part, they would sooner wrestle with tigers than lead us up the slopes.

There was no arguing the point—they were beyond reason. Nevertheless, in the face of common sense, I could not be contented. From the beginning, that womanlike image had taken hold of my imagination; and, far from discouraging me, the fears and protestations of the natives had only whetted my curiosity. Should opportunity offer, I would scale the mountain and discover for myself if there was any excuse for that terror which the stone figure aroused in the Afghans.

The opportunity, unfortunately, was not long in coming. That evening we pitched camp among the pines at the base of "The Mountain of Vanished Men." Since the site was ideally located at the brink of a clear-bubbling rivulet, and since several of us were exhausted from our strenuous traveling, we decided to remain for a day or two before continuing toward the northern gorges.

Next morning I urged that, whether with guides or without, several of the men join me in a climb to the stone image. The ascent, I pointed out, promised to be easy enough, for the mountain showed a long even grade that rarely approached the perpendicular; and, in the absence of undetected glaciers or ravines, there would be nothing to keep us from the peak. I was even so confident as to assert that, starting shortly after dawn, we would set foot on the summit and be back in camp by evening.

Most of my comrades were not convinced. They swore that it would be foolhardy to entrust ourselves to this unknown wilderness; they painted in gruesome terms the danger of being lost, and the still greater danger from wild beasts, rock slides, and crevasses in the snow and ice; and they scoffed when I vowed that I would go alone if no one would accompany me.

Yet among our party there was one who, either through lack of foresight or an insensitiveness to fear, was ready to risk any hazards. That man, Jasper Damon, was one of those persons with a passion for getting into trouble,—a sure instinct for upsetting canoes in deep water, or invading hollow tree trunks infested with rattlesnakes. All through this expedition he had been my especial companion; and now, while the others sat by with loud guffaws and mocking grimaces, he rushed to my rescue. Springing from his seat just when I most needed an ally, he shook my hand and assured me that a little jaunt to the top of the mountain was the very thing he desired.

Even today I do not know why he joined me. Perhaps the figure on the peak exercised a mysterious compulsion upon him, as upon me; or perhaps he was merely moved by good fellowship. But, whatever his motives, he displayed real zest in his preparations. His black eyes fairly crackled in his long, stubbled face; his lean, lanky figure, with the spidery legs, bustled about in noisy animation. In less time than it took me to make the proposal, he had secured food and firearms and a knapsack containing ropes and climbing equipment; and, scornful of the warnings of our companions and the oaths and mutterings of the natives, he started with me on the long ascent before the sun had lifted its head halfway above the east-ridges.

For more than an hour we plodded along a vague little trail beneath the dark foliage. Many a day must have passed since the last man had followed this track; the occasional small five-clawed footprints showed who the recent passers-by had been. But we were not depressed by thought of the frightful solitudes, nor by fear of the unseen creatures occasionally rustling in the brush; and even when we had literally to dig our way through the thickets, we did not let discouragement mar our spirits. Although the slopes were moderately steep, they were not hard to scale; and we felt sure that early afternoon would see us on the summit.

This hope found support when, before the morning was half over, we reached a more sparsely timbered area, and shortly afterwards came out into a region of straggling shrubs. The rocky ribs of the mountain now stretched bare and gigantic before us, the dismal gray slopes inclining at an angle of from twenty to fifty degrees. Far above, perched on a little cone not unlike the tip of a volcano, that curious statue-like formation loomed encouragingly larger; and a wisp of cloud dangled playfully about the summit and beckoned us to be of good cheer and make haste.

But it was not easy to make haste along those unsheltered ridges under the glaring mid-July sun. More than once, as Damon and I sweltered upward, we glanced regretfully back at the green valley; and more than once we observed that the peak, like the fruit of Tantalus, seemed only to retreat as we toiled to approach it.

The higher we mounted, the less likely did it appear that we could gain the summit and return by evening. We encountered no impassable obstacles, and never had to use the climbing tackle; yet in places we literally had to crawl, relying upon our arms as much as upon our legs, and consequently were so delayed that when the sun stood in mid-heaven the peak still beckoned from the remote blue.

Had any trace of our wits remained, we would now have recognized that we sought the unattainable. But that inscrutable figure above had woven a charm about us; upward, still upward we trudged, pausing only for an occasional drink from an icy little stream. Our eyes were so fascinated by the peak, and by its amazing woman-shaped crown, that we did not notice signs which could hardly have escaped us in a more cautious mood. Not until too late did we observe the increasing murkiness of the atmosphere, the gradual formation of bands of mist that gathered as if from nowhere, the merging of those bands into clouds that obscured the further ranges and approached us with silent and deceptive velocity.

I was just speculating as to the distance still before us, when an exclamation from Damon startled me back to reality. And suddenly I was aware of the menace.

The skies were no longer blue, but gray with vapor; the slopes below us were disappearing in fog, and even the peak was being blotted from view!

"Back! Let's go back!" I muttered, thoroughly frightened.

Without a word, Damon joined me in frantic retreat.

But we had delayed too long. Before we had returned many hundred yards, the fog was all about us. Like some evil unearthly thing, it blocked our pathway with intangible streamers, and reared a gray wall before us and to every side, and stretched a gray roof just overhead; and it drew closer, insidiously closer, until we could see not ten feet beyond, and the wild panorama of the mountains had given way to a hazy cell the size of a small room.

A cautious man, no doubt, would have proposed remaining where we were. But neither of us relished the prospect of camping possibly for twenty-four hours in this solitary spot; and both of us vaguely felt that, after descending a little, we would come out into the daylight beneath the clouds. Besides—and this was most unreasonable, and most unlike me—I was agitated by a dim, superstitious fear, I could scarcely say what of, as if by some sixth sense I knew of shadowy horrors that lurked unseen and unheard in the gloom.

Yet we had to advance with the timidity of tight-rope walkers; at any instant, we might find ourselves dangling at the edge of a precipice. In the first moments of that unequal contest we had hopelessly lost our way; we had been unable to follow the trail, since we could not see far enough to recognize the landmarks; while, as we descended at random among the rocks, we realized that, even should we escape from the fog, we might find it far from easy to make our way back to camp.

I do not know how long we continued groping through the mist. It may have been half an hour, or an hour; certainly, it seemed the better part of a day. But as Damon and I picked our path between the boulders among the enfolding vapors, despair was gradually settling over us both, and we felt as if some malign spirit had walled us off from the world.

Even so, I cannot explain how we opened the door for the greatest horror of all. Perhaps it was only that Damon was displaying his usual recklessness; perhaps that the fog had driven us in too much upon ourselves. All I know is that, looking up after an absent-minded revery, I received a bewildering shock—the mist was hemming me in almost at arm's length, and Damon was not to be seen!

For a moment I was too dazed to cry out. My mind was filled with the fantastic ideas that come to a man at such a crisis. Had my companion stepped over a precipice? Had he been crushed by a dislodged boulder? Had some prowling beast fallen upon him?

As these questions shot over me, I was startled to hear my name shouted in a familiar voice. But the words seemed to issue from far away, and I had only the vaguest idea of their direction.

"Damon! Damon!" I shouted back, in mingled hope and dismay. "Where are you?"

"Here! Here, Prescott! Here!" came the voice, after a second or two. But I was still mystified as to the direction.

Yet, in my excitement, I cried, "I'm coming!" and started off on what I imagined to be the proper course.

At intervals the calling continued. Damon's voice did not seem to draw nearer, but did not seem to grow more remote; and several times, by way of desperate experiment, I changed my direction—which only increased my confusion. Now I would be sure that the voice cried from my right, and now that it shrilled from my left; at first I thought that it came from beneath me, but before long I felt that its source was above.

And as I went fumbling through the fog, anxiety gave way to panicky impatience, and the slim remnants of my wits deserted me. The climax came when, after forcing my way through a cluster of jagged rocks that bruised my arms and legs and tore my clothes, I found myself at the base of a cliff that shot upward abruptly out of sight. From somewhere above, I felt sure, I heard Damon's voice calling, hoarse from overstraining and plaintive with fear. And at the thought that an unscalable wall divided us, I behaved like a trapped animal; heedless of the abysses beneath, I started hastily along the base of the cliff in what I supposed to be Damon's direction.

But again I had miscalculated. When I next heard my friend's voice, it was much fainter … growing ghostly faint and remote; and continued to grow fainter still, until it was no more than a murmur borne across far distances. And now, when I screamed his name in a cracked and broken way, the only answer was in the echoes that reverberated along the mountainside, with thin and hollow notes like the mockery of fiends.

In despair, I told myself that I had lost track of Damon completely. But all at once a resounding report broke the stillness of the mountains. Shocked, I stood as if frozen—and instantly the report was repeated. Was Damon battling some foe, four-footed or human? Or was he merely signaling with his revolver?

Then, while I stood quivering there beneath the precipice, the pistol rang forth again, and again; and the echoes pealed and dinned with unearthly snarls and rattlings.

So unnerved was I that I did not think of replying with my own revolver. But, seized with a frenzy to rejoin Damon at all costs, I started through the fog almost with the madness of a stampeding steer.

And now at last my recklessness betrayed me. Whether my foot slipped, or whether I had dared an impossible grade, I do not know; but with breathless suddenness, I was plunging down a terrifying slope. To stop myself was beyond my power; with a sprinter's speed I went racing down the mist-dimmed mountainside. For an instant I had visions of gigantic spaces beneath me, of prodigious chasms, jutting rocks—then all things grew blurred, my mind whirled round and came to a stop ... and the darkness that ensued was for me as the end of the world.

CHAPTER II
THE VERGE OF THE PRECIPICE

Hours must have passed while I lay without movement or consciousness. For when at length I came to a confused awareness of myself, the scene had changed alarmingly. The fog must still have been about me; but all that met my eyes was a black blank, an opaqueness so absolute that for the moment I imagined I had lost my sight. It was a minute before I dimly recollected what had happened, and knew that I was somewhere on the mountainside, and that it was now night.

But it was long before I realized the full horror of my predicament. My head was feeling dull and dazed; my throat was parched; I was by turns shivering and burning, and my limbs were all aching and sore. I was lying sprawled head down on a couch of rock, and a rock-wall to my left formed my support and pillow; but when I tried to change position, a staggering pain in my right arm warned me to go slowly, and I understood that the limb was hanging limp and useless.

It did not occur to me then to wonder what had happened to Damon, nor how long I should have to remain here, nor how I should escape. My thoughts were blurred and half delirious, and I think that unconsciousness came to me again in snatches. More often than not I was as one in a dream; visions of white peaks beset me continually, and always on those peaks I saw a gigantic woman with hands outspread and beatifically smiling face; and that woman seemed at times to call to me, and at times to mock; and now she would take me to her in great warm arms, and now would vanish like vapor in my clasp....

It was after one such nightmare that I opened my eyes and found the darkness less intense. A pale gray light seeped wanly through the mist; and in that dreary dawn I came gradually to understand my own helplessness. While everything above was clouded, the fog had unrolled from below—and my gaze traveled to panoramas that bewildered and appalled me. Then, as by degrees the fumes cleared from my mind, I was able to realize just what had happened—and shuddered to think what might have happened. I was resting on a narrow ledge; above me the rocky grade leaned at an angle halfway to the vertical, and beside me was a blood-spattered boulder. It was this obstruction that had saved my life—directly at my feet, a precipice slanted down to the dim depths.

And yet, as I lay there groaning, I wondered if I would not have been better off to have plunged into the chasm. I was so bruised that I could hardly move a limb; my legs were too feeble to support me when I strove to rise; internally I was so shaken that I could not be certain of my equilibrium; and my right arm, acutely painful, dangled helplessly at my side. Clearly, escape would be impossible....

And if at first I imagined that there was just a chance of rescue—just a chance that a searching party from camp would find me—my hopes gave place to a dull, settled despair as the hours wore endlessly away. The fog, after lifting for a while, slowly re-formed; and with its return I felt that my death-sentence had been passed. I could not now be seen at more than twenty yards—and who could come near enough to discover me on this detached shelf?

There followed an interval in which I must have sunk into delirium. Then, after a series of grotesque imaginings or dreams in which I was always trying to drink from streams that vanished at my touch, I was roused from a half-conscious lethargy by the sound of voices. Could it be that I was still dreaming? As eagerly as was now possible, I stared into the wilderness of crags. The fog had vanished; but the only moving thing was a great bird circling in the blue.

Cruelly disappointed, I again closed my eyes. But once more I thought I heard voices calling. This time there could be no doubt—the sound had been clear-cut, reminding me of men joyously shouting.

And as that sound was renewed, I opened my eyes again, and peered searchingly into the abyss. Still all was bare and motionless. Yet, even as I wondered, I heard those mysterious voices anew, nearer now than ever; and for the first time I recognized that they came not from beneath me but from above! Eagerly I gazed up at the rocky heights—but there was no sign that they had ever been disturbed by human presence.

I was half convinced that my fever had been playing me tricks, when a slender little moving shape far above caught my attention. After an instant, it disappeared behind a ledge, but after another instant emerged; and close behind it trailed other specks—slowly jogging specks with upright forms!

In that first dumbfounded moment, I did not ask myself who they might be. Enough that they were human—and almost within hail! Quivering uncontrollably, I strove vainly to lift myself to a sitting posture. Then, with what scanty lung power remained to me, I attempted to shout; but my dry throat gave forth scarcely a feeble mumbling, the mere ghost of a voice.

And directly following that first sharp relief, still sharper terror seized me. Must I remain here unseen? At that thought, I was racked with a dry crackling laugh, more like a cough than an expression of mirth; and I lifted my left hand and frantically waved my red-bordered handkerchief, while cackling and gibbering to myself like an insane old man.

By bending my neck and straining my eyes, I could still follow the figures. Had my enfeebled voice permitted, I would have shouted out curses, would have laden them with all the imprecations of hell, when they passed directly above and glided on their way around a bend in the mountain. There were at least half a dozen of them, and they could not have been from the camp, for they were clad in blue and red not at all like the khaki we wore; and their voices had some quality quite unlike anything I had heard before. There even seemed to be a note of excitement in their calls, a tone of surprise, though of that I could not be sure.

Some time later I opened my eyes once more, and saw three turbaned men descending almost within arm's reach.

Whether they had been friends or head-hunting savages, their first effect upon me would have been the same. In my weakened state, I was unprepared for the shock; my senses forsook me, and unconsciousness returned.

But when at length I came to myself, I seemed to be in another world. The first thing I realized was that I was sitting with head propped up against the boulder; and at the same time I was aware of the sound of voices, voices that were pleasant although unfamiliar. And as I opened my eyes, my surprise increased; not three strangers but six stood before me, two of them women!

Even in my half-dazed condition, I observed something peculiar about these persons. A single glance told me that they belonged to no race I had ever seen or heard of; they were manifestly mountaineers, yet did not wear the usual Afghan garb. Men and women alike were attired in stout loose-fitting dark-blue garments of some material reminding me of canvas, with red stripes and dots, and bizarre yet not unattractive designs. In person they were clean-cut and prepossessing; the men tall and well-built, with long full beards, swarthy countenances and proud flashing black eyes; while the women were among the most attractive I had ever seen.

So, at least, it seemed to me when the younger, scarcely more than a child, lifted a small leather flask to my mouth and motioned me to drink.

With an effort, I moistened my lips; then, frantic as a drug addict deprived of his drug, I swallowed a long draught, draining the entire contents.

And as, half revived, I lay against the boulder, I observed that the strangers were all peering at me with curiosity and wonder. But equal wonder and curiosity, I am sure, stared from my own eyes; while my glance may have already been too partial to her who had ministered to my thirst. For I could see how strikingly she differed from her companions; her complexion was lighter than theirs, and she had an airy grace and beauty which set her apart.

Peering at her closely, I thought that she might be about sixteen or seventeen. Her clear white skin had the stainlessness of perfect health; her hair, which hung in unbound curls and ringlets about her slender neck, was of a rich auburn; her eyes, in startling contrast to that auburn, were dark like the eyes of her kindred, and in the deep brown of the iris live fires glowed and smoldered; her features were modelled with exquisite daintiness, the forehead of medium height and rounded like a half moon, the nose small and gracefully pointed, the gently curving chin tapering to a firm little knob. Her lips, tiny and thin, had at times a creasing of merriment about the corners that gave her almost a puckish appearance. Although slimly built and not much over five feet in height, she did not lack at all in robustness; she flitted from place to place with great agility; and her rude unhampering garments fitted her ideally for mountain climbing.

After the exhaustion of our first few minutes together, I was again close to unconsciousness. But now I felt strong hands lifting me; and opened my eyes to find two men smiling upon me encouragingly. At the same time, something pungent and aromatic was thrust between my lips; the girl was extending a handful of dried herbs, which she motioned me to consume with a genial dimpling smile that I had no power to resist.

After swallowing the food, I felt considerably better. Having finished the entire handful and washed it down with a draught from a second leather flask, I had revived sufficiently to try to sit up unaided; and simultaneously I realized how ravenously hungry I was, and felt a fresh desire to live flaming up within me.

Being eager for a word with my benefactors, I muttered something in English without thinking exactly what I was saying. But the surprised answering stares cut me short in sharp realization. What could these mountain folk know of English?

There was a short, awkward pause; then, after a few words among themselves, they addressed me in their native tongue. At the first syllable, I realized that theirs was not the cultivated Persian of the Afghan court, but rather a variety of Pushtu, the speech in most common use among the people. From my wanderings of the past few months and especially from contact with the native guides, I had gathered a few words of this language, enough to enable me to recognize its peculiar intonation, although I could express none but the simplest ideas.

After a second handful of the dried herbs, and another draught of water, I felt well enough to try to stagger to my feet. But the effort was too much for me; my limbs threatened to collapse beneath me; and two of the men had to bolster me up.

But once I had arisen, they would not let me return to my rock-couch. Grimly they motioned toward the snow-streaked northern peak, as if to indicate that we must pass beyond it; at the same time, one of them pointed to the stone image on the summit; while the others, as if observing a religious rite, extended their arms solemnly and almost imploringly toward that strange womanly figure.

At the moment, it did not occur to me that their attitude was one of prayer; but later I was to remember this fact. For the time, my thoughts took a more personal turn; for when I saw my new acquaintances preparing to lead me across the mountains, I was profoundly alarmed. Although still too stunned to take in the full reality, I knew that I was on the threshold of unpredictable adventures, and that many a day might pass before I could rejoin my fellow geologists.

But when the ascent actually began, I was not at all certain that I should survive. We seemed to be undertaking the impossible; I had, literally, to be lifted off my feet and carried; my legs were useful only on the short stretches of comparatively level ground. In the humiliation of being an invalid, I felt a deep sense of inferiority to these brawny men that tugged and strained to bear me up the mountain; while, with increasing admiration, I noted the capable way in which they carried me along the brink of canyons, or over grades that I should have had to make on my hands and knees. But greatest of all was my admiration for the young girl who had offered me the dried herbs. She seemed agile as a leopard and sure-footed as a mountain sheep, leaping from boulder to boulder and from crag to crag with the swiftness and abandon of a joyous wild thing....

Hours—how many I cannot estimate—must have been consumed in the ascent. Fortunately, I am not a large man, being but five feet six in height and considerably under the average weight; but, even so, I proved more than an ordinary burden. Though my rescuers worked in shifts and each seemed powerful enough to carry me single-handed, yet before long the exertion began to tell upon them all. Occasionally, after completing some precipitous ascent, they would pause to mop their brows and rest; or else their bulging eyes and panting frames would testify to the ordeal they were undergoing.

Higher and higher we mounted, while they showed no thought of abandoning their efforts. In joy not unmixed with a half-superstitious dread, I saw the statuesque figure on the peak slowly approaching; saw its outlines expand until it seemed but a mile away, clad in a somber gray and beckoning like some idol superbly carved by a race of Titans. But while I was asking myself whether we were to climb to the very foot of this image, I observed that we were following a little trail which no longer ascended but wound sinuously about the mountainside. For what seemed time unending we plodded along this path, while in my weakness I was more than once close to fainting.

But, as we jogged ahead, the scenery was gradually changing; from time to time I caught glimpses of far-off snowy peaks and a deep basin north of "The Mountain of Vanished Men." It was long before this valley stretched before us in an unbroken panorama; but when I saw it entire it was enough to make me forget my sufferings.

Certainly, it was unlike any other valley in the world. A colossal cavity had been scooped out in the heart of the wilderness; on every side the mountain walls shot downward abruptly for thousands of feet, forming a circle dominated at all points by jagged and steepled snow-tipped peaks. Dense woods mantled the lower slopes, and the valley's entire floor was forested except for relatively small patches of grass lands. The whole depression might have been five miles across, or might have been fifteen; but it was deep and round as the crater of some gigantic extinct volcano; and there seemed to be scarcely a pass that gave exit or ingress. I particularly noticed how the shadows, creeping blackly from the western mountain rim as the afternoon sun declined, shed an uncanny, ghost-like effect; while remote waterfalls, leaping soundlessly from the high cliffs with slender streamers of white, served only to enhance the impression of a spectral and unreal beauty.

It was with sudden joy that I saw my new-found acquaintances turn toward this valley, and realized that this was the home to which they were leading me.

CHAPTER III
WELCOME TO SOBUL

How we accomplished the descent is one of the mysteries that will always be associated in my mind with the Valley of Sobul. Even for the unhampered traveler, as I was to learn, the grades were perilous; but for climbers impeded with the weight of a disabled man, they must have been well-nigh impossible. Unfortunately, I have little recollection of what happened on the way down; I believe that I was half delirious from hunger and pain; I have indistinct memories of muttering and screaming strange things, and at best I can recall that we trailed as in a dream along endless spiral paths by the brink of bottomless chasms.

It was late twilight when I was aroused to a dim awareness of myself. Evidently our party had halted, for I was lying on the ground; on all sides of me, unfamiliar voices were chattering. Although still too listless to care much what happened, I opened my eyes and observed a crowd of dusky forms moving shadow-like through the gloom. In their midst, perhaps a hundred paces to my right, a great golden bonfire was blazing, casting a fantastic wavy illumination as it glared and crackled; and by its light I thought I could distinguish a score or more of little cabin-like structures.

In my feverish state of mind, I had the impression that I had been captured by savages; tales of cannibals and cannibal feasts, in a nightmarish sequence, streamed across my memory. Perhaps I cried out in a half-witted way; or perhaps it was merely that I groaned unconsciously at my wounds, for suddenly I found myself the focus of attention for the dusky figures; a dozen pairs of eyes were peering at me curiously. Among them were two which, even in the dimness, I thought I could recognize:

while the multitude were mumbling unintelligibly, a feminine form bent over me, and a feminine voice murmured so gently that I was reassured even though I did not understand the words.

And again I felt myself lifted by strong hands; and, after a minute, I was borne through a doorway into the vagueness of some rude dwelling. The room was a small one, I judged; in the sputtering candlelight it appeared to me that my outspread arms could have reached halfway across. Yet I took no note of details as the unseen hands placed me on a mass of some stringy, yielding substance. So exhausted was I that I quickly lost track of my surroundings in much needed sleep.

It may have been hours before I awoke, greatly refreshed, yet with a sensation of terror. All about me was darkness; the silence was complete. For an instant I had an impression of being back on the mountain in the fog; then, as recollection came flashing upon me, I understood that I was safe among friends. But all the rest of that night I was tormented by dreams of lonely crags and mantling mists; and when again I awoke it was abruptly and after a nightmare fall over a precipice whose bottom I never reached....

To my joy, it was once more twilight. By the illumination of an open, glassless window, I could distinguish the details of the room—and singular details they were! The walls were of logs, great rough-hewn pine logs standing erect and parallel, with the bark still clinging; slenderer logs formed the flat low ceiling; and timbers crudely smoothed and levelled constituted what passed for a floor. Scattered masses of straw did duty as a carpet, while straw likewise composed my couch; and I was lying so low that I could have rolled to the floor without injury. I noted that the room had neither ornament nor furniture; that the wide, open fireplace, filled with cold ashes, seemed almost the only convenience; and that the door, while as massively built as the walls, was apparently without lock or bolt.

But as the light gradually increased, it was not the room itself that held my attention, but rather the view from the window. No painting

I had ever observed was so exquisite as that vision of a green and white eastern mountain, rounded like a great head and aureoled with rose and silver where the rays of sunrise fought their way fitfully through serried bands of cloud.

The last faint flush had not yet faded from above the peak when the cabin door creaked and slowly opened, and I caught a glimpse of auburn hair, and saw two brown eyes peering in at me curiously. A strange joy swept over me; and as the fair stranger stood hesitating like a bashful child in the doorway, my only fear was that she would be too timid to enter.

But after a minute she overcame her shyness; gently and on tiptoe she stepped in, closing the door carefully behind her. I observed that she had not come empty-handed; she carried not only a water-jug but several odd little straw-colored objects. Approaching slowly, still with just a hint of hesitation, she murmured pleasantly in the native tongue; then, having seated herself cross-legged on the floor within touching distance, she offered me the water, which was crystal-clear and cool. The eagerness with which I drank sent a happy smile rippling across her face; and the daintiest of dimples budded on both her cheeks.

After I had satisfied my thirst, she held out one of the straw-colored objects invitingly. I found it to be hard and gritty of texture, like some new kind of wood; but while I was examining it, turning it round and round like a child with a new toy, my visitor was pointing to her open lips, and at the same time revolved her gleaming white teeth as though chewing some invisible food. I would have been dull indeed not to understand.

A single bite told me that the object was a form of native bread. The flavor of whole wheat was unmistakable; and, to my famished senses, it was the flavor of ambrosia. Only by exercising unusual will power could I refrain from swallowing the loaf almost at a gulp.

My greedy disposal of the food was evidently reward enough for my hostess, who beamed upon me as if well pleased with herself. I even thought—and was it but imagination?—that her shy glances were not purely impersonal. Certainly, there was nothing impersonal in the stares with which I followed her every motion—or in my disappointment when after a time the great log door swung inward again to admit a second caller.

Yet I did my best to greet my new visitor with signs of pleasure; for I recognized him as one of my rescuers. He entered as silently and cautiously as though on his best sick-room behavior; and after peering at me curiously and returning my nod of welcome, he murmured a few words to the girl, and as silently and cautiously took his leave.

Thenceforth, I was to receive visitors in a stream. The moments that day were to be few when three or four natives were not whispering in a corner of the room. A census of my callers would have been a census of the village; no one able to stand on his own legs missed the opportunity to inspect me. Children of all ages and sizes appeared in groups; gaped at me as if I had been a giraffe in a menagerie; and were bustled out by their elders, to be followed by other children, by men in their prime, women with babes in arm, and tottering grayheads. But most of my hosts showed that they were moved by warmer motives than curiosity; many bore offerings of food and drink, fruit and berries, cakes and cereals, bread and cheese and goats' milk, which they thrust before me with such generosity that I could consume but a small fraction.

While they swarmed about the cabin, I observed them as closely as my condition permitted. Their actions and garb made it plain that they were peasants; all, like yesterday's acquaintances, were dressed in rude garments of red and blue, with colored turbans and striped trousers and leggings, the feminine apparel differing from the masculine chiefly in being more brilliant-hued. And all, men and women alike, were robustly built and attractive. The majority had handsome, well modelled faces, with swarthy skins and candid, expressive eyes, at the sight of which I felt reassured; for here in the mountains of Afghanistan, among some of the fiercest and most treacherous tribes on earth, I might easily have fallen into less kindly hands.

During the day I was visited by two men who took a particular interest in me. The first, who came early in the morning, was evidently the local equivalent of a physician, for he examined me from head to foot with a solemn and knowing air and caused me much annoyance by feeling my limbs as if to see that they were whole. Of course, he did not overlook my right arm; and I passed a miserable half hour while he adjusted a crude splint and bound and bandaged the broken member with stout vegetable fibres.

My second visitor performed less of a service. He was an old man, still erect and sparkling-eyed, although he must have passed the traditional three score years and ten; and his long white beard, drooping untended as far as his waistline, gave him a Rip Van Winkle appearance. Upon his entrance, the others made way with little bows of awe; and as he sedately approached the straw where I was lying, five or six men and women gathered to my rear, whispering in half-suppressed agitation. These were quickly joined by others from without; and soon my visitors were massed layers deep against all the walls, and the air became fetid and hot with overcrowded humanity.

Meanwhile I felt like a sacrificial victim awaiting the priestly knife. Had my hosts spared me only so that I might serve as an offering to some pagan god? So I wondered as I watched the white-bearded one gravely bending over me; watched him rubbing his hands solemnly together as though in pursuance of a religious rite. And when, after several minutes, he turned from me to smear a brown ointment on his palms, my apprehension mounted to terror, which was not soothed when he stooped down and dampened my forehead with the ointment, meanwhile mumbling unintelligibly to himself. His next step, which I awaited in the trembling helplessness of a vivisected animal, was to reach toward my clothes and examine them fold by fold; after which he drew from his pocket a sparkling object, a prism of glass, which he held up in the sunlight of the window, shedding the rainbow reflection on the opposite wall, and staring at it as though it were the key to some transcendent truth.

Much to my relief, the ordeal was apparently over now; the old man turned his back upon me as though I had ceased to matter, and began sonorously to address his people. Not understanding a word, I could not be much interested; but I did observe how reverentially his audience stood regarding him, with staring dark eyes and gestures of self-abasement, while hanging on his every syllable as if it embodied divine wisdom.

His first remarks were evidently cheerful or even jocular; for they evoked smiles and occasionally laughter. But soon, apparently, he turned to graver subjects; and his listeners became serious and thoughtful, as though spellbound by his eloquence. How long they remained thus I do not know; my watch having run down, I had no way of reckoning time; but it seemed to me that the speaker held forth for at least an hour. And long before he had finished, my mind had drifted to more interesting matters.

I was asking myself what had happened to Damon, and whether my fellow geologists were searching the mountains for my corpse, when the old man wheeled about abruptly, and with fiery eyes pointed at me as if in accusation.

In high-pitched, staccato tones, almost like a cry of agony, he uttered three sharp monosyllables, then became silent.

At the same time, suppressed cries burst from the spectators. It may have been only imagination, but I thought they were eyeing me in alarm and reproach, and that they were edging away from me; and I know that, in a moment, those to the rear had crowded through the door. Soon only three or four remained, and I was left to wonder whether my rescuers were after all not the kindly mountaineers I had taken them to be, but merely superstitious savages.

CHAPTER IV
THE WEAVING OF THE SPELL

For more than five weeks I lay on my sick-bed, at first close to death, then slowly convalescing. After my rescue and temporary revival, a raging fever had attacked me; and I have little recollection of what followed, except that it was a nightmare of blurred impressions. Among my jumbled memories of those days when I lay balanced on the borderline, there is only one image that stands forth distinctly: the picture of a great pair of smoldering brown eyes surmounted by auburn curls and ringlets. Curiously enough, that picture became associated in my mind with visions of paradise. At times, for rare brief snatches, it seemed as if I were surrounded by that heaven in which I had long lost faith, and as if the possessor of the brown eyes were a ministering angel. Around her there seemed to be a light, as of some celestial presence; and when she went away she left only darkness and vacancy. Other forms there were, of course, other forms ceaselessly coming and going, coming and going, moving on tiptoe, silent or whispering like conspirators. But these were mere shadows in a void, grotesque or cloudy thin or unreal, the monstrous creatures of a world I had almost ceased to inhabit.

Perhaps it would have been well if I had indeed ceased to inhabit this world. Certainly, it would have been well for one whose tragic eyes come before me even now, haunting me like a ghost and looking reproach at every line I write. But that is to anticipate; destiny works in circuitous ways; and I, the stranger in the Vale of Sobul, could not have known that my arrival was to weave a fatal spell over her whom of all the world I should least have wished to injure.

But no such gloomy thoughts obsessed me as by degrees my fever subsided and the clouds lifted from across my mind. Even in my feebleness and dependence upon strangers, I could see cause for thanksgiving; once more I felt that the world was a bright place, and life worth living. Perhaps I would have thought otherwise had it not been that every day, in the early dawn and then again at sunset-time, an auburn-haired visitor came to attend me. Always she would bear some offering, sometimes merely a flask of spring water, sometimes some dainty morsel of food, more often a spray of wildflowers with which she would decorate the cabin walls. Although many of her tribesmen visited me frequently, supplying me with all physical necessities, her arrival was the one event of importance; and the long waking hours became tolerable and even pleasant through the thought of her.

Our relations, fortunately, were not long confined to the stares and gestures of our first acquaintanceship. Realizing that I desired to speak with her, and encouraged by finding that I already knew a few words of Pushtu, she set about to teach me her language; and every day, for half an hour or more, she transformed herself from the smiling friend into the solemn instructress, first teaching me the local term for every visible object, and then linking the words together to form simple sentences. As her tutorship was ably furthered by her tribesmen, it was not long before I had mastered a vocabulary of all the more common words; and since I amused myself during my spare hours by repeating these words mentally and combining them into phrases, not many days had passed before I could speak Pushtu at least as well as a five-year-old.

And what a joy when at last I could converse! Merely to exchange the simplest ideas with my friend was delight enough! But all the while there had been questions that I had been burning to ask, and now one by one I could ask them! No longer would that lovely creature be nameless to me—she confided with a blush that she was called Yasma, and was the daughter of Abthar, the vine-grower. As for her people—they were the Ibandru, a tribe which from the beginning of time had inhabited the Valley of Sobul, tilling the land for its rich harvests but finding their chief joy in roving the mountainsides. But who her people were and whence they were descended Yasma could not tell me; she could only say that they possessed the valley undisputed, and had little intercourse with other tribes; and she related for me an ancient legend that the first of her people had been born of the nuptials of the south wind and the spring flowers, so that the spirit of the flowers and of the wind must breathe through the tribe forever.

Naturally, I was less interested in such myths than in facts touching upon my own predicament. I was curious as to all that had occurred since my rescue from the mountain ledge; and was particularly anxious to know the meaning of that strange scene with the white-bearded seer on my first day in Sobul. And to most of my questions I received an answer, although not always one that satisfied me. My rescue was explained simply enough: the Ibandru habitually roamed the mountains for miles around their valley, and a party of six had been going in search of a little blue stone which one of their sages had declared to exist upon the higher slopes, and the possession of which would mean happiness. With their trained eyes accustomed to scanning the far distances, they had observed what they at first took to be some peculiar animal crawling along a ledge; and, drawn closer by curiosity, had discovered that the supposed animal was human, and was in distress. Common humanity dictated that they come to the rescue, bear me to safety, and house me in an unoccupied cabin whose owner (to use the native phrase) had gone "beyond those mountains that no man crosses twice."

Thus far I saw no reason to doubt the explanation; but when I mentioned the white-bearded tribesman I could see that I trod upon questionable ground. It was not only that Yasma hesitated before answering; it was that she replied with a nervous, uneasy air. She informed me—and this much was certainly true—that the old man was Hamul-Kammesh, the soothsayer, whose wisdom was held in high esteem; and she stated that, immediately following my arrival, he had been called upon to judge of the signs and omens. But what had he said? She refused to tell me. Or, rather, she told me with transparent dissimulation. She declared that he had prognosticated something of good, and something of evil; and her reluctant manner testified that the evil tipped the balance of the scales. But just what evil did he imagine my coming might do? And to whom would the damage be done? No matter how I pleaded and questioned, Yasma shook her head sadly, and refused to reply.

Could it be that the prophecy concerned me in some vital way? that it would endanger me, or make my lot harder to bear? Yasma was still sphinx-like. "I cannot answer," she maintained, in response to all my entreaties. "I cannot." And biting her underlip, she remained resolutely silent.

But I could not accept her refusal. "Why cannot you answer?" I insisted. "Surely, there is nothing to fear."

"That you cannot know," she sighed, her lips compressed as though in suffering, and an unexplained sadness shining from her eyes.

Then, seeing that I was about to return to the assault, she disarmed me by murmuring, resignedly, "Well, if I must tell you, I must. You see, it is not this prophecy alone. This only confirms another—another prophecy made years and years ago. And that first prediction was dark as a night-cloud."

"Dark—as a night-cloud?" I asked, noting that her beautiful rounded cheeks were becoming drawn and blanched, while a light of fear and agony, a light as of a hunted creature, was shining in her eyes.

"Yes, dark as a night-cloud," she muttered, mournfully. "But more than that I cannot say." And then, as if afraid that she would say more despite herself, she flitted to the door, and with a whispered "Good-bye!" was gone, leaving me amazed and angry and yet just a little overawed, as if in defiance of reason I recognized that my coming had cast a shadow over the homes of my hosts.

CHAPTER V
YULADA

I t was indeed a happy day when I regained the use of my legs and staggered out of my log prison.

Now for the first time I saw the village of Sobul. It was composed of several scores of cabins like that in which I had been confined; and these were sprawled over a broad clearing, separated from one another by considerable spaces. Beyond the furthest houses the open fields stretched on all sides for half a mile or more, some of them tawny brown with the ripening wheat, or green with flourishing herbs in long tilled rows; while herds of half-wild goats browsed among the meadows, and gnarled old orchard trees stood in small groves varied by grapevines scrambling over mounds of earth.

Further still, at the ragged rim of the fields, the forest encroached with its dense-packed legions; and I observed where in the background the woods began to rise, first gently, then with a determined ascent, until they clung to the precipitous and beetling mountain walls. And higher yet there were no trees, but only bare rock, crags like steeples or obelisks or giant pointing hands, and crowded peaks with fantastic white neckbands. It was with awe that I discovered how completely these summits hedged me in, confining me at the base of the colossal cup-like depression. And it was with something more than awe—with amazement mingled with an indefinable shuddery feeling—that I noted a familiar figure perched on a dominating southern peak. It was that same womanlike stone image which had lured me almost to death: with hands uplifted, and one foot upraised, she stood as when I had seen her from the other side of the mountain. If there was any difference in her aspect it was scarcely noticeable, except that she now seemed a little more elevated and remote.

What was the meaning of the statue-like form? I would inquire at the first opportunity; and that very day, accordingly, I spoke my mind to Yasma. But again she was to fail me. Like the Afghan guides, she was reluctant to discuss the subject; her lips wrinkled with a faint displeasure, and her eloquent dark eyes were averted. Only upon being urgently pressed would she answer at all; and then, from her hasty attempts to change the subject, I judged that she knew more than she wished to admit; I suspected that she was just a little shocked and frightened, almost like a pious lady tempted into a profane discussion.

But her resistance merely whetted my curiosity. And at length I coaxed her into a partial explanation.

"There is a story among our people," she said, while her eyes took on an unusual gravity, "that five thousand years ago the gods placed that stone image on the peak to watch over us and guide us. Yulada we call her, a name given by the early seers of our tribe. So long as we obey Yulada's wishes, she will bless us and bring us happiness; but if we forget her commands, she will scourge us with earthquake and lightning."

Upon uttering these words, Yasma startled me by stooping toward the floor, bending her neck low as if in supplication, and mumbling a series of apparently meaningless phrases.

"Then the stone image is some sort of god?" I questioned.

Yasma continued muttering to herself.

And as I stood watching in perplexity, I was enticed once more by that same rash idea which had almost cost my life. "Sometime I'm going up to Yulada," I vowed, my curiosity piqued to the utmost. "Then I'll find out for myself what's she's like."

An expression of alarm, almost of horror, distorted the clear, mobile features.

"Oh, you must not!" she cried, interrupting the ceremonies, and resuming an erect attitude. "You must not ever, ever go up to Yulada!"

"Why not?"

"None of our people," she explained, hurriedly, and still with that look of fright, "must ever go within five stones' throws of Yulada. It would be terrible, terrible to go too close!"

"But why?"

She hesitated, in pitiable uncertainty; then hastily narrated, "Long, long ago our soothsayers foretold that great sorrow would come to whoever climbed within touching distance of the stone woman. And so, in fact, it has proved to be. Only three men, within living memory, have ever defied the warning; and all have learned the way of bitter wisdom. One fell to his death in a crevasse of the mountain, and one was bitten by a serpent and perished in agony, and one lost his wife and first-born son, and passed the rest of his days in loneliness and despair."

Yasma paused again, sadly as though brooding on some personal grief; then passionately demanded, "Promise me, promise that whatever happens, you will never, never go up to Yulada!"

In her voice there was such pleading, and in her face such pain, that I had to make the promise. Yet I am ashamed to say that, even at the time, I suspected that I should not abide by my word.

Meanwhile the mystery of Yulada was not the only shadow that had thrust itself across my mind. As I gradually regained the use of my limbs, I began to be troubled by thoughts of the future; I recognized how great was my debt to the natives; and was ashamed at thought of accepting their hospitality without making any return. Yet the prospects were that I should remain with them for more than a few days or weeks. My fellow geologists had doubtless given me up long ago as lost; and there was no telling how many months would pass before I could find my way out of this wilderness. To attempt to wander unguided among the mountain labyrinths would be suicidal; and I not only had no way of knowing how far it was to the nearest civilized settlement or trade route, but could obtain no information from my hosts. Reluctantly I admitted to myself that I was marooned.

And although the spell of Sobul was already upon me, I was not so captivated that I did not dream of escape. True, it would have caused me a pang to leave the kindly mountain folk, and particularly Yasma, but what could this count against my life-work, the remembrance of my friends in America, and all the arts and allurements of civilization?

Yet what could I do to escape? After long reflection, only one project had occurred to me—and that unpromising enough. Though the other geologists had certainly gone long ago, might they not have left some message for me in the hope that I was yet alive? Yes, even a message instructing me how to escape? Meager as the chances were, would it not at least be worth while to revisit the site of our former camp?

Somewhat doubtfully, I consulted the natives. But they regarded my suggestion as quite natural, and several volunteered to accompany me across the mountains as soon as I was strong enough.

It was early September, more than seven weeks after my arrival in Sobul, when at last I was ready for the expedition.

Accompanied by three of the Ibandru, I started out along a slender trail that ran straight toward the jutting northern slope of "The Mountain of Vanished Men." But these three were quickly increased to four; we had hardly started when an auburn-haired girl came tripping behind us, joining us in defiance of the scowls of the men. For my own part, I was far from displeased at her presence; with her gleaming eyes to encourage me, I found it just a little easier to accomplish the abrupt and perilous climb. And both perilous and abrupt it was, for when we were not crawling on hands and knees up gigantic broken natural stairways of rock, we were winding single-file in long horseshoe curves between a precipice and a cliff, or skirting the treacherous verge of a glacier.

Straight up and up we went, for hours and hours, until we stood but a few hundred yards below the great stone image, which loomed mighty as a hill, like some old Egyptian colossus magnified many times and miraculously transported to the mountain top. When we had approached our nearest to it, we came to a halt and the natives dropped to the ground and swayed their arms toward it as though entreating a favor. Then, mumbling solemnly, they continued on their way around the mountain, and the stone figure gradually dwindled and retreated.

Now from time to time we caught glimpses of the southern valley, another bowl-like hollow scooped out in the core of the mountains. It was with mixed emotions that I observed this spot where I had bidden my friends farewell—farewell for how long? And it was with the return of an unreasoning horror that I surveyed those very slopes where I had been imprisoned in the fog. Yet I was eager to descend, so eager that several times I forgot caution in my impatience; once one of the men jerked me back violently as I set foot on a stone which gave way beneath me and went hurtling down a thousand feet; and once Yasma caught my arm as something long and shiny unwound itself from beneath my feet and disappeared hissing among the rocks.

But though I drew upon every particle of my energy, I was so slow that frequently the others had to pause and wait for me along the steep, narrow trails; while occasionally they helped me over a difficult slope. Because I was the weakest of the party, it was I that set the pace; and consequently our expedition was protracted hours beyond their reckoning. Even though we had set out at dawn and stopped but a few minutes to consume some fruit and small native cakes, sunset found us only at the timber line of the second valley.

Here we had to make camp; and here we dined sparingly from the provisions carried by my guides, quenched our thirst from a clear, swift-running stream, built a campfire, and prepared for our night on the open ground. Shortly after dark I noted that Yasma was no longer among us; but when I questioned the men they appeared unconcerned, replying that she knew how to take care of herself.

This statement proved true enough; the first thing I was aware of, after a chilly and restless night, was the sound of Yasma's voice. She had come with the earliest birds to awaken us; and, herself like a bird in the lithe grace with which she tripped and fluttered about, she urged us to be up and starting almost before the last golden embers had turned ashen above the eastern semi-circle of peaks.

My whole being was in a tumult as we set forth, for it seemed to me that today was to decide my fate. Should I receive some word from my friends, some clue to guide me back to civilization? Or should I find myself abandoned in the wilderness? An hour or two more should tell the tale, since already we had discovered the winding little path Damon and I had followed on our fateful expedition.

But as we glided silently in single file along the trail, I felt hope dying within me. All things about us seemed deserted; scarcely a living creature could be heard amid the dense brush; scarcely a dead leaf stirred, scarcely a bird chirped or twittered. It was as if I had invaded a realm of the dead, a realm of specters and shadows.... By the time we had reached a remembered pine-grove beside a clear-bubbling rivulet, I was almost in a despondent mood, which was only accentuated when I observed that the grove was forsaken. Yet how well I recalled the enthusiasm with which Damon and I had set forth from this very spot!

While Yasma and the men waited cross-legged on the ground, I began carefully to explore the grove. Actually, I expected to find nothing, and at first I found what I expected. Then one by one I came across various relics, insignificant in themselves, which pained me like the opening of old wounds. First it was merely a bent and rusting tin; then the ashes of a campfire, a scrap of old newspaper, the stub of a cigarette, or a broken penknife clinging to the bark of a tree; and, finally, a half-used and forgotten notebook and pencil, which I picked up and bore away for possible future needs.

But was this to be all? In my dejection, I was almost persuaded so, when my eye was caught by a pile of stones at one end of the former camp. It was between two and three feet high, pyramidal in shape, and clearly of human workmanship. Eagerly I inspected it, at first without understanding its purpose, but with swiftly growing comprehension. Carved indistinctly on one of the stones, in small barely legible letters, were the words, "Look below!"

In a frenzy, I began tearing the stones aside, casting them in all directions in my haste.

Yet at first I discovered nothing—nothing! It was only after careful examination that I espied, between two stones in a protected position, a little scrap of ink-marked paper.

Like one receiving a message from another world, I grasped at the paper. The scrawled handwriting was that of Jasper Damon!

It was a minute before I could choke down my excitement sufficiently to read:

"Dear Prescott: I am leaving this note with hardly any hope that you will find it, or that you are not now beyond the reach of all human messages. I cannot believe that you have been spared, for after losing you in the fog and failing to reach you by shouts and pistol signals, I have discovered no sign that you still live. For my own part, I had to pass the night between two sheltered rocks on the mountainside; but, luckily, I was unhurt, and when the fog lifted for a while the next morning I managed to make my way down below the mist-belt. Then, after wandering for hours, I fell in with a searching party from camp. I was alarmed to learn that they had found no trace of you, and more alarmed when, after searching all the rest of the day, we were still without any clue. On the following morning we made a much wider hunt, and bribed and intimidated the native guides to lead us up the mountain, which they feared and hated. Still no results! You had vanished as completely as the very fog that hid you—on the next day, and still on the next we scoured the mountains, always in vain. For a week now we have lingered here, until hope has disappeared, and, in deepest sorrow, we must continue on our way.

"But while reason tells me that you have perished, I cannot keep back a vague feeling that somehow you escaped. It is merely out of a whim, and in spite of the smiles of our skeptical friends, that I am building this mound of stones to draw your attention if ever you return, and hiding this letter so that if need be it may withstand the elements for years. It will do you little enough good, but at least you will have learned that we did not willingly desert you. How you will be able to struggle out of this wilderness is a question that heaven itself may not be able to answer—I can only pray that some fortunate chance may save you as it has saved me.

"Farewell, Dan Prescott!—You cannot know how every day of my life will be overshadowed by thought of that foolhardy escapade of ours.

"Your wretched friend,

"Jasper Damon."

CHAPTER VI
FORESHADOWINGS

I t was in a bitter mood that I trudged back to Sobul. Even the mirth and laughter of Yasma could not dispel my gloom; I was as one who has seen a black vision, one who has read the handwriting on the wall. It seemed to me that my life had reached a barricade as formidable as the mountain bulwarks that hemmed me in; there was no longer a straw to clutch at; I was irredeemably a prisoner. Only once on the return trip did I break my silence, and that was to ask, as I had done a thousand times, what roads led back to trade routes, navigable rivers, or civilized settlements; and it was no consolation to be told, as invariably before, that there were no roads; that Sobul held no intercourse with the world, and that I was the first of my race ever seen there. I realized, of course, that there were rude trails leading out, for had not the Afghan guides escorted our geologists to this vicinity? Yet none of the Ibandru seemed to know anything of such trails, and how find my way unaided?

Then I must spend the winter with the Ibandru! In a few weeks the snow would be piling on the high mountain shoulders, and winter would hermetically seal the Valley of Sobul until the approach of April.

Meanwhile, as I have mentioned, another problem had been troubling me: that I had been a drone living off the hospitality of the Ibandru, consuming their hard-earned provisions while making them no return. Hence I thought of consulting their chieftain, in order to arrive at some way of earning my board.

On the day after returning to Sobul, accordingly, I asked Yasma who was the leader of her people.

"Leader? There isn't any exactly," she replied, looking troubled. "That is, not any regular picked person. We are all free to go our own way, and if anyone breaks any of our laws or customs his punishment is set by a council of all the tribe."

"But is there no one whose word has particular authority?"

"Yes, in a way there is," she admitted, thoughtfully. "Whenever the people want advice, they look first to my father, Abthar. And next, they turn to the soothsayer, Hamul-Kammesh."

I had seen the soothsayer, and conceived a hearty dislike for him. But I thought it would be a good idea to meet Yasma's father.

Therefore I made a simple request, which seemed to please the girl. With a happy smile she led me out among the fields, and into the thick of vines mounted on trellises or sprawling over mounds of earth, where a gaunt tawny-browed man was busy plucking the purple clusters of grapes. I had already seen him several times; more than once he had visited me when I lay ill, bringing offerings of food and drink; and I had noted that the other men had greeted him with deference. But I had not known him then as the father of Yasma. Now, spurred on by my new information, I scrutinized him as never before: the tall agile form, unstooped and vigorous although he must have seen sixty summers; the sagacious lean face, dominated by long black hair crossed by steely bars, and terminating in a beard of black and gray; the glittering alert brown eyes, which shone proudly as an eagle's and yet not without a softness that reminded me of Yasma herself.

At my approach he arose with a cordial smile and reached out both hands by way of greeting (a salutation peculiar to the Ibandru). In a few words Yasma mentioned that I had a message for him; and while she started back to the village, he motioned me to be seated on the ground beside him.

"What is it that you wish to tell me?" he asked kindly, and sat staring at me with an intent, inquiring air.

In a fumbling manner, I explained that I could not return to my people at least until next year, which would force me to continue to accept his people's hospitality. But I did not wish to impose upon their kindness; and was anxious to make myself of use in the village.

With an impassive silence that gave no clue to his thoughts, Abthar heard me to the end; and then answered unhesitatingly and with dignity.

"The views you express, young man, do you great credit. But we Ibandru desire no return for our hospitality, and still less for what we do out of simple humanity. Say no more about the matter. You owe us no debt; we shall be glad to have you remain as long as you wish."

I scarcely knew how to reply, for the old man arose as if to dismiss the subject. But I would not be turned aside. After thanking him for his kindness, I reminded him that there was a long winter to come; and insisted that I did not desire to be a drain upon his people's supplies.

At mention of the winter, a peculiar light came into Abthar's eyes—a light that I thought just a little ironic, just a little pitying, and at the same time just a little wistful. I may merely have imagined this, of course; but in view of what was to come, I am persuaded that I did not imagine it. And even at the time, though still unacquainted with the ways of the Ibandru, I wondered if the winter had not some queer significance for the tribe. For not only was Abthar's expression extraordinary, but he repeated several times, slowly and as if to himself, "The winter, yes, the winter—we must remember the winter."

Unfortunately, I did not put the proper interpretation upon Abthar's words—how possibly interpret them correctly? I assumed that the cold season in Sobul must be particularly rigorous, or must be invested with superstitious or religious importance. Hence I failed to ask questions that might have proved enlightening.

"Then the winter here is a difficult time?" was my only answer to Abthar's muttered half-reveries.

"You may indeed find it so!" he returned, his big deep-brown eyes snapping with a peculiar force. And then, after a pause, he continued, again with that pitying air I could not understand, "I am glad, young man, that you mentioned the winter. I think you had better make ready for it, since—who knows?—you may find it hard to bear."

"Well, after all," I argued, "I have been used to cold weather in my own country."

"It is not only the cold weather," he assured me. "But wait and learn—you may not even feel the winter. Yes, you too may escape the barren and frozen days."

"Why should I escape any more than anyone else?"

But he did not reply, and I thought it fruitless to pursue the discussion. As yet I had had little reason to suspect that the Ibandru were not as the other tribes huddled among the fastnesses of the Hindu Kush; and, in my ignorance, I overlooked completely the meaning behind his meager, succinct phrases. And so, instead of attempting to fathom a mystery, I turned the conversation into practical channels, and asked just how to prepare for the winter.

"You can discover that for yourself," said Abthar, picking his way as if pondering an unfamiliar problem. "First of all, you must fill in your cabin window with a thick covering of dead boughs, and must cement all the cracks and empty places with clay, so as to hold out the blizzards. Then you must make yourself a cloak of goat's hide, and also must gather firewood, storing as much as possible within your cabin, and much more just outside. The most important thing, however, will be to provide food, for the cold months may be long, and you may be unable to find a crumb to keep you from starving."

Not until long afterwards did I remember that Abthar had spoken as if I were to lead a hermit's life. At the time, I was too deeply absorbed in my own thoughts to see beyond his words; the question of how to obtain sufficient food was occupying me almost to the exclusion of other subjects, and I contented myself with asking how to earn my winter's board.

"You need not earn it," asserted Abthar, frowning. "Must I remind you again that hospitality is not a lost virtue among the Ibandru? Merely go out into the fields and take what you want—all the grain you can bear away, apples from our orchards, plums and grapes for drying, nuts from our groves, beets and pumpkins and whatever vegetables our farms produce."

Again I thanked Abthar—and again expressed my unwillingness to take so freely.

"You will be accepting nothing that we need," he insisted. "No matter how much you require, we will have ample."

And with a nod signifying that the interview was over, Abthar returned to his work amid the vines.

Hence it came about that, during the following weeks, I was busy preparing for the winter. Under the warm September skies, flecked with scarcely a cloud and lying like a serene blue roof between the great pillars of the peaks, I was providing ceaselessly for the season of tempests and snow. I equipped my cabin to be snug and relatively weather-proof; I heaped it with firewood in the shape of the sawed dead pine-branches which I bore laboriously from the forest; I provisioned it with lentils, millet, wheat, barley, beans, dried mushrooms, and "salep" (a paste made from a local tuber), which the people showered upon me with amazing generosity.

But do not imagine that I found this work distasteful. City-bred modern though I was, I felt a certain atavistic joy in my return to the primitive. That joy, I must confess, was all the greater since I did not always labor alone, for Yasma, like an agile and ingratiating child, frequently would come running to my assistance. Not only did she prove a fascinating companion, but she would display remarkable skill and strength at manual tasks; she would insist on lifting great chunks of firewood, yet would scarcely appear to feel the strain; she would pile my provisions in a corner of the cabin with a regularity and neatness that made me marvel; she would bring me earthenware pots and pans, jugs and kitchen utensils, and would seem to hear neither my protestations nor my thanks.

Nevertheless, I was already beginning to observe—and to be puzzled at—the contradictions in her manner. Although she freely volunteered to help me, she did not always work wholeheartedly. At times there was a sadness and constraint about her; and my most determined efforts could not penetrate behind the veil. Even today I can see her standing aloof and wistful in the green fields, gazing in a revery toward the great stone woman on the peak, or merely following with her eyes the lazily drifting cotton clouds as though she would float with them to lands beyond the mountains. I do not know why this memory comes back to haunt and mock me, for then I did not understand, and now that I understand it is too late; but when I recall how she would remain staring at the southern summits, it seems to me that her eyes were like the eyes of fate itself, peering beyond that which is to that which must be and that which never can be.

But not always was she in so somber a mood. Frequently, like a nimble-footed child, she would go tripping with me to the forest, where we would collect the fallen dead branches; and she would flit about happily as a fairy when we would gather pine-nuts, or pluck grapes or apples, or search for mushrooms, or dig in the fields for edible roots. It would be as though for a moment she had cast off a shadow—but for a moment only, since always the shadow would return.

One sure way of bringing the oppression back was by asking a certain question that was puzzling me more and more. While I was preparing so laboriously for the winter, I was amazed to note that I was alone in my efforts. No one else appeared aware that winter was coming: no one filled in the gaps in the cabin walls, or made the windows storm-proof; no one wove heavy clothing, or obtained more than the day's firewood, or more food than seemed required for the moment's needs. At first I had muffled my surprise by telling myself that soon the Ibandru would begin their preparations; but as the days went by, and the unharvested grain-lands lay tawny and dry, and the forest began to be flecked with crimson and russet and yellow, a strange uneasiness laid hold of me, and my growing astonishment was tinged with an unreasoning fear. Ponder as I might, I could find no explanation of the Ibandru's seeming negligence, particularly in view of Abthar's advice; and from the Ibandru themselves I could expect no enlightenment. Always, when questioned, they would evade the issue; they would tell me to wait and be assured of an answer from heaven; or they would point mutely and mysteriously to Yulada, as though that were a self-evident solution.

Even Yasma failed me despite repeated questionings. When I referred even casually to the winter, she would assume that meditative and far-away expression which I detested so heartily because it seemed to make her so remote; a deep melancholy would shine in her eyes, and she would peer at me with a vague unspoken regret. But she would never admit why she was melancholy; and would answer me only indirectly, in meaningless phrases. And at length, one evening in late September, when I questioned her too persistently, she turned from me in a sudden torrent of tears.

Reluctantly I had to acknowledge my defeat, and to confess that, whatever mysteries might lurk behind the mountains of Sobul, I should have to wait in silence until time should make all things plain.

CHAPTER VII
YASMA

E ven before I began to succumb to the mysteries of Sobul, the country was captivating me with a subtle spell. There seemed to be something magical about the noiseless atmosphere, the untroubled blue skies and the aloof calm circle of peaks; I came almost to feel as if this were the world and there were no universe beyond; and my memories of the years before were becoming remote and clouded as memories of a dream.

But the enchantment of Sobul was not merely the wizardry of its woods and open spaces, its colors and silences and eagle heights. There was a more potent sorcery of twinkling eyes and caressing words that was fettering me in soft, indissoluble bonds—a sorcery that might have proved powerful in any land on earth. And the priestess of that sorcery was Yasma. Perhaps she did not realize the fateful part she was playing, for was not she, as I, swept along by a dark current there was no resisting? And yet she enacted her role remorselessly as though assigned the lead in a cosmic drama; and, blinded herself by the unseen powers, she could not have realized how certainly and how tragically she was intertwining her fate with mine.

From the first I had been charmed by her open manner and her evident lack of self-consciousness. She had been free as a child in talking and laughing and romping with me, and I had tried to think of her as a child, and little more,—undeniably a fascinating playmate, but certainly not a serious companion for a thirty-three-year-old geologist. But if I had imagined that I could dismiss her so easily, I was merely deluding myself;

the time was to come, and to come very swiftly, when I should realize how much more than a child she was.

Possibly it is that the girls of the Ibandru come early to maturity; or possibly they do not labor under civilized repressions, and are seldom other than their natural selves. At all events, Yasma suffered from few of those inhibitions which would have hampered her western sisters. Finding something in me to interest her, she was at no pains to conceal her interest, but would act as unhesitatingly as if she had been the man and I the woman. At first, during my illness, I had attributed this to mere kindness; later I had ascribed it to a natural curiosity as to a stranger from a strange land; but there came a time when I could no longer believe her motives purely impersonal, and when, while knowing that she acted without design, I had inklings that she was rushing with me toward a fire in which we might both be singed.

Why, then, did I not try to forestall our mad dash toward the flames? Surely I, who was older and more experienced, was also somewhat wiser; surely I might have prevented complications that she could not even foresee. Ah, yes!—but love has queer ways, and makes a jest of men's reason, and tosses their best intentions about like spindrift ... and I was but subject to the frailties of human-kind. Writing at this late date, I find it hard to say just why I did what I did (even at the time, would I have known?); and it is impossible to explain why she did what she did. But let me recount a few incidents; let me describe as well as I can the growth of that strange, wild love, which even now torments me in recollection.

I particularly remember one afternoon when we sallied off into the woods together, on a sort of frolic that combined work and play, to gather the wild walnuts that grew abundantly in those parts. It was Yasma that suggested the expedition, and I had been quick to accept the proposal, which had brought back memories of boyhood "nutting parties" among the New Hampshire hills. As we set out through the forest on a little inconspicuous trail, it was indeed delightful to be together; and for the moment I was almost ready to bless the fate that had sent me to Sobul.

What a rare companion she made that day! She would go darting and tripping ahead of me like a playful wild thing, and then, when I had lost sight of her amid the underbrush, she would startle me with a cry and would come running back in loud laughter. Or else she would enthusiastically point out the various trees crowded together in that virgin forest—the sedate oaks, the steeple-like deodars and pines, the alder and the ash, the juniper and wild peach; or, in places where the undergrowth was dense, she would show me species of wild rose and honeysuckle, of currants and hawthorn, of gooseberry and rhododendron, as well as of a score of native herbs whose names I have forgotten. Or her sharp eyes would spy out the birds' nests in the trees (nests that my untrained vision would never have detected), or she would call attention to some gray or blue or red-breasted moving thing, which would flash into view and slip away like some shy phantom into the twilight of the vines and shrubbery or amid the light-flecked, latticed roof of green. Occasionally, when not too busy dancing along the trail or playing some merry prank or pointing out the shrubs and flowers, she would sing a snatch of some native song— sing it in an untrained voice of a peculiar sweetness and power, which affected me strangely with its note of joy tinged always with an indefinable and haunting melancholy.

At length, after perhaps an hour of this careless adventuring, I noticed that the ground was beginning to rise sharply, and judged that we were not far from the valley wall. And it was then that Yasma paused, clapping her hands in delight and pointing to a cluster of big, gracefully rounded trees, whose nature I recognized immediately, although their pinnate leaves were broader than those of the black or American walnut and their trunks were smoother and not so intensely brown.

Beneath the trees, which were already tinged with the buff and yellow of autumn, I drew forth two large fibrous bags supplied by Yasma, and began to collect the nuts that lay scattered on the ground. But she, with a disapproving gesture, halted me. Almost before I could guess her intentions, she had sprung cat-like up one of the trees, and sat perched acrobatically among the middle branches. Then, while I stood gaping at her in amazement, I became aware of a storm amid the foliage. The boughs began to shake as if in a tempest, and dead and half-dead leaves drifted down to the accompaniment of a shower of little missiles.

Half an hour later, after Yasma had raided a second tree and I had collected all the nuts I could carry, we sat side by side with our backs against a tree-trunk, recovering from our exertions. I cannot say why, but, in contrast to our previous exuberance, a silence had fallen over us; we each seemed wrapped up in our own thoughts, almost like strangers who have never been introduced. What was passing through her mind I shall never know; but, for my own part, I was noticing as never before what an extraordinarily fascinating girl Yasma was; how utterly unspoiled, with a wild blossoming beauty that would have made most fair women of my acquaintance seem paper roses by comparison. A warm, romantic desire was taking possession of me, a desire such as I had not known for years and believed I had outgrown—a desire to take Yasma in my arms, and hold her close, and whisper tender, meaningless things. And while I was repressing that longing and telling myself what a fool I was, an insidious question wormed its way into my mind: what if I were to marry this girl, and take her away with me to civilized lands, and surround her with the graces and refinements she could never have among these remote mountains? As one dreams of paradise and rejects the dream, so I thought of linking Yasma's life with mine, and thrust the idea aside. Imagine trying to civilize this wild creature, this creature with the ways of the deer and the dove!

In the midst of my reveries, I was startled by hearing Yasma's voice. "Strange," she was saying, in low thoughtful tones, "strange, isn't it, how you came here to us?"

"Yes, it is strange."

"And stranger still," she continued, as much to herself as to me, "how little we know of you now that you are here. Or, for that matter, how little you know of us."

Then, turning to me with a sudden passionate force, she demanded, "Tell me, tell me more about yourself! I want to know more—to know more about you!"

Often before she had asked such a question; but never with quite the same eagerness. On the former occasions I had replied briefly, with a vagueness half forced upon me by my poor knowledge of the language; but now I saw that I must answer in detail. It would not do to state, as previously, that I came from a land beyond the wide waters, where the cities were high as hills and the people many as flies in autumn; and it would not suffice to explain that I had passed my days in acquiring dark knowledge, knowledge of the rocks and of things that had happened on earth before man came. From her earnest, almost vehement manner, it was clear that Yasma would not be put off with generalities, but wished to know of intimate and personal things.

Picking my way cautiously, I answered as well as I knew how. I told of my boyhood in New England; of how I had wandered among the stony hills, interested even then in the rocks; of how my father and mother had sent me to a great university, where I had studied the earth's unwritten story; of how I had been a teacher in that same university, and later a member of the scientific staff of a famous museum, by which I had been sent on expeditions into the far places of the world. These and similar facts I reported to the best of my ability, finding it difficult if not impossible to express my meaning in the simple Pushtu vocabulary. But while Yasma listened as well as she was able, she did not appear satisfied. I might almost say she did not even appear interested, for often her face expressed a total lack of comprehension.

It may have been after ten or fifteen minutes that she broke in impatiently, "That's all very well, what you are saying—all very well. But you are not telling me about yourself—this might all be true of a thousand men. What is there that's true only of you? What are you like deep down? What do you think? What do you feel? Oh, I know you cannot explain outright—but do say something to show what you are like!"

"You put a hard question," I objected, just a little embarrassed. "I simply don't know how to answer."

And then, as a pleasant means of shifting the burden, I suggested, "But maybe you'll show me how, Yasma. Maybe you'll show me by telling something about yourself."

"Do you really want to know?"

"There is nothing that interests me more."

"Very well," she assented, after an instant's hesitation. "I will tell you from the beginning."

And, with a reflective smile, she related, "I was born here in the Valley of Sobul, seventeen summers ago. I have two brothers and three sisters—but I won't say anything about them, because you're going to meet them some day. When I was born, a strange prophecy was made by the soothsayer, Hamul-Kammesh"—here she paused, and the trace of a frown came over her face—"but I won't say anything about that, either."

At this point, of course, I interrupted and insisted on knowing about the prophecy, which, I suspected, was connected with the prediction she had already mentioned. But she would neither confirm my surmise nor deny it.

"When I was five summers old," she went on, "I suffered a great misfortune. My mother, whom I remember only as a kind spirit who came to me long ago in a dream, was taken away by the genii of the wind and snowstorms, and went to live with the blessed ones on the highest peak of that range which meets the stars. Ever since that time, I have been lonely. I have often stood looking up above our tallest mountains, up above Yulada to the mountains of the clouds, and wondered if she might be there, gazing down and hearing the prayers I spoke to her in my heart. But she never seemed to see me, and never seemed to hear. And as I grew up, my brothers and sisters would go off playing by themselves, and I would be left to myself—but I would not always care, for I loved to be alone with the mountains and trees. I would go chasing butterflies all afternoon; or I would scramble up the mountainside, picking wild fruits and berries and laughing to see the little squirrels go jumping out of my path; or I would watch the clouds riding through the sky, and imagine that they were fairy boats bearing me away to strange and wonderful lands. But sometimes I would be frightened, when I heard some big beast rustle in the bushes; and once I saw the face of a great staring black bear, and ran down the mountain so fast I nearly fell over a cliff; and once I almost trod on a coiling snake, but the good spirits of the mountain were with me, because if it had bitten me you would not see me now."

Yasma paused, a dreamy glow in her lustrous brown eyes. And before she could continue I put a question which, I fancied, might shed a ray on some perplexing problems.

"You are telling me only about the summers. How was it in the wintertime, when the blizzards shrieked and the snow fell, and you were cooped up in your log cabin?"

It seemed to me that a curious light, half happy and half melancholy, came into her eyes as she murmured, "Ah, the winters, the winters—until now I have never worried about them. They were always the best time of all."

"Why the best time?"

She merely shook her head. "I cannot tell you," she answered, regretfully. "You would not understand."

Yes, indeed, there was much that I did not understand! Even to discuss the matter brought a cloud between us; her manner grew unnatural and constrained, as if she had something to conceal and was anxious to change the subject. To press her would only have ended all conversation for the day; and so, after vexing myself fruitlessly, I abandoned the discussion, although with a deepened sense of something sinister and mysterious about the Ibandru, something somehow connected with the seasons of the year.

"Come, tell me more about your past," I requested, reverting to our original topic. "Have you always been so solitary? Have you had no companions?"

"I have always had companions, but have always been solitary," she declared, as though unconscious of the paradox. "Yet what are companions if you cannot tell them what is in your heart? What are companions if you stand looking with them at the sunset, and you feel its loveliness till the tears come, and they feel nothing at all? Or what are companions if you watch the birds twittering in the treetops, and are glad they are living and happy, while your friends wish to mangle them with stones, and laugh at your softness and folly? I would not have you think that we Ibandru are of the kind that would harm little birds; only that my kinsmen and I do not have the same thoughts. I suppose it is my own stupidity and strangeness that makes all the difference."

"No, your own natural wisdom makes all the difference."

"I wonder," she mused, as she absently toyed with the decaying dead leaves that coated the rich dank soil. "I have tried to be like the others, but never could be. I would always speak about things they did not seem to understand; and they would jest about things that were sacred to me. I would be interested in the bee and the grasshopper, the crawling little worm and the bird that flies like the storm-wind; but they would not care, and would not often join me in my rambles through the woods, for I might pause too long to make friends with some new flower, or to watch the ants as they swarmed into one of their wonderful earthen houses. Oh, they are marvelous, the things I have seen! But the others have not seen them, and think me queer for noticing them at all!"

"Never mind, Yasma," I whispered, consolingly. "I do not think you queer. I think you clever indeed."

"Oh, I'm so glad!" she cried, clapping her little hands together happily. "You're the first who ever said that!"

"Come, come now, certainly not the first," I denied. "Surely, some of the others—say, your father—"

"No, not father! He's very, very good to me, of course, but he's like all the men—imagines that the great god of the flowering spring, and the god of the ripening fall, who put women into the world, had only one use for them. And he thinks I'm growing old enough to—"

Abruptly Yasma halted, as though she feared to tread on unsafe ground. Her fingers still fumbled among the dead leaves, while her averted eyes searched the dense, dark masses of foliage as if in pursuit of something elusive and much desired.

"But I've told you enough about myself," she resumed, hastily, in a half whisper. "Now it's your turn to speak about yourself."

Though I would have done all I could to please her, I was still at a loss for a reply. Embarrassed at my own speechlessness after her frank recital, I wasted much time in telling her that I really had nothing to tell.

"Oh, yes, you must have," she insisted, almost with a child's assurance, as she looked up at me with candid great brown eyes. "What friends had you before you came here? Had you any family? Were you always alone, as I was? Or were there many people around you?"

"Yes, there were many people," I declared, hesitatingly, "though no one who was close of kin, and no one who was such a comrade to me as you have been, Yasma. No, never anyone at all. I did not have any lovely young girl to help me and be kind to me and go romping into the woods with me for nuts and berries."

I paused, and noted that Yasma sat with eyes still averted, still gazing into the shadowy thickets as if she saw there something that interested her immensely. And as I peered at the delicately modelled features, the sensitive nostrils and lips and the auburn hair heaped over the rose-tinged cheeks, I seemed to detect there a wistfulness I had never noticed before, an indefinable melancholy that made her appear no longer the dashing, tumultuous daughter of the wilderness, but rather a small and pathetic creature pitifully in need of comfort and protection. And at this thought—purely fanciful though it may have been—my mind was flooded with sentiments such as I had not known for years. Spontaneously, as though by instinct, my hand reached out for hers, which did not resist, and yet did not return my pressure; and my lips phrased sentiments which certainly my reason would have countermanded if reason had had time to act.

"You don't know what a beautiful girl you are, Yasma," I heard myself repeating the old commonplace of lovers. "What a rare, beautiful girl! I have never known anyone—never—"

"Come, let us not talk of such things!" Yasma cut me short. And she leapt to her feet with a return of her former animation. "See! the sunset shadows are already deepening! In another hour the woods will be cold and dark!"

Again the impetuous wild thing, she seized one of the bags of nuts before I had had time to stop her, and went darting off before me along the forest track, while I was left to follow slowly in a sober mood.

CHAPTER VIII
THE BIRDS FLY SOUTH

t was early in October when the mystery of the Ibandru began to take pronounced form.

Then it was that I became aware of an undercurrent of excitement in the village, a suppressed agitation which I could not explain, which none would explain to me, and which I recorded as much by subconscious perception as by direct observation. Yet there was sufficient visible evidence. The youth of the village had apparently lost interest in the noisy pastimes that had made the summer evenings gay; old and young alike seemed to have grown restless and uneasy; while occasionally I saw some man or woman scurrying about madly for no apparent reason. And meantime all bore the aspect of waiting, of waiting for some imminent and inevitable event of surpassing importance. Interest in Yulada was at fever pitch; a dozen times a day some one would point toward the stone woman with significant gestures; and a dozen times a day I observed some native prostrating himself in an attitude of prayer, with face always directed toward the figure on the peak while he mumbled incoherently to himself.

But the strangest demonstration of all occurred late one afternoon, when a brisk wind had blown a slaty roof across the heavens, and from far to the northeast, across the high jutting ridges of rock, a score of swift-flying black dots became suddenly visible. In an orderly, triangular formation they approached, gliding on an unwavering course with the speed of an express train; and in an incredibly brief time they had passed above us and out of sight beyond Yulada and the southern peak. After a few minutes they were followed by another band of migrants, and then by another, and another still, until evening had blotted the succeeding squadrons from view and their cries rang and echoed uncannily in the dark.

To me the surprising fact was not the flight of the feathered things; the surprising fact was the reaction of the Ibandru. It was as if they had never seen birds on the wing before; or as if the birds were the most solemn of omens. On the appearance of the first flying flock, one of the Ibandru, who chanced to observe the birds before the others, went running about the village with cries of excitement; and at his shouts the women and children crowded out of the cabins, and all the men within hearing distance came dashing in from the fields. And all stood with mouths open, gaping toward the skies as the successive winged companies sped by; and from that time forth, until twilight had hidden the last soaring stranger, no one seemed to have any purpose in life except to stare at the heavens, calling out tumultuously whenever a new band appeared.

That evening the people held a great celebration. An enormous bonfire was lighted in an open space between the houses; and around it gathered all the men and women of the village, lingering until late at night by a flickering eerie illumination that made the scene appear like a pageant staged on another planet. In the beginning I did not know whether the public meeting had any connection with the flight of the birds; but it was not long before this question was answered.

In their agitation, the people had evidently overlooked me entirely. For once, they had forgotten politeness; indeed, they scarcely noticed me when I queried them about their behavior. And it was as an uninvited stranger, scarcely remembered or observed, that I crept up in the shadows behind the fire, and lay amid the grass to watch.

In the positions nearest the flames, their faces brilliant in the glow, were two men whom I immediately recognized. One, sitting cross-legged on the ground, his features rigid with the dignity of leadership, was Abthar, the father of Yasma; the other, who stood speaking in sonorous tones, was

Hamul-Kammesh, the soothsayer. Because I sat at some distance from him and was far from an adept at Pushtu, I missed the greater part of what he said; but I did not fail to note the tenseness with which the people followed him; and I did manage to catch an occasional phrase which, while fragmentary, impressed me as more than curious.

"Friends," he was saying, "we have reached the season of the great flight.... The auguries are propitious ... we may take advantage of them whenever the desire is upon us.... Yulada will help us, and Yulada commands...." At this point there was much that I could not gather, since Hamul-Kammesh spoke in lower tones, with his head bowed as though in prayer.... "The time of yellow leaves and of cold winds is upon us. Soon the rain will come down in showers from the gray skies; soon the frost will snap and bite; soon all the land will be desolate and deserted. Prepare yourselves, my people, prepare!—for now the trees make ready for winter, now the herbs wither and the earth grows no longer green, now the bees and butterflies and fair flowers must depart until the spring—and now *the birds fly south, the birds fly south, the birds fly south!*"

The last words were intoned fervently and with emphatic slowness, like a chant or a poem; and it seemed to me that an answering emotion swept through the audience. But on and on Hamul-Kammesh went, on and on, speaking almost lyrically, and sometimes driving up to an intense pitch of feeling. More often than not I could not understand him, but I divined that his theme was still the same; he still discoursed upon the advent of autumn, and the imminent and still more portentous advent of winter....

After Hamul-Kammesh had finished, his audience threw themselves chests downward on the ground, and remained thus for some minutes, mumbling unintelligibly to themselves. I observed that they all faced in one direction, the south; and I felt that this could not be attributed merely to chance.

Then, as though at a prearranged signal, all the people simultaneously arose, reminding me of a church-meeting breaking up after the final prayer. Yet no one made any motion to leave; and I had an impression that we were nearer the beginning than the end of the ceremonies. This impression was confirmed when Hamul-Kammesh began to wave his arms before him with a bird-like rhythm, and when, like an orchestra in obedience to the band-master, the audience burst into song.

I cannot say that the result pleased me, for there was in it a weird and barbarous note; yet at the same time there was a certain wild melody ... so that, as I listened, I came more and more under the influence of the singing. It seemed to me that I was hearing the voice not of individuals but of a people, a people pouring forth its age-old joys and sorrows, longings and aspirations. But how express in words the far-away primitive quality of that singing?—It had something of the madness and abandon of the savage exulting, something of the loneliness and long-drawn melancholy of the wolf howling from the midnight hilltop, something of the plaintive and querulous tone of wild birds calling and calling on their way southward.

After the song had culminated in one deep-voiced crescendo, it was succeeded by a dance of equal gusto and strangeness. Singly and in couples and in groups of three and four, the people leapt and swayed in the wavering light; they flung their legs waist-high, they coiled their arms snake-like about their bodies, they whirled around like tops; they darted forward and darted back again, sped gracefully in long curves and spirals, tripped from side to side, or reared and vaulted like athletes; and all the while they seemed to preserve a certain fantastic pattern, seemed to move to the beat of some inaudible rhythm, seemed to be actors in a pageant whose nature I could only vaguely surmise. As they flitted shadow-like in the shadowy background or glided with radiant faces into the light and then back into the gloom, they seemed not so much like sportive and pirouetting humans as like dancing gods; and the sense came over me that I was beholding not a mere ceremony of men and women, but rather a festival of wraiths, of phantoms, of cloudy, elfin creatures who might flash away into the mist or the firelight.

Nor did I lose this odd impression when at intervals the dance relaxed and the dancers lay on the ground recovering from their exertions, while one of them would stand in the blazing light chanting some native song or ballad. If anything, it was during these intermissions that I was most acutely aware of something uncanny. It may, of course, have been only my imagination, for the recitations were all of a weird nature; one poem would tell of men and maidens that vanished in the mists about Yulada and were seen no more; another would describe a country to which the south wind blew, and where it was always April, while many would picture the wanderings of migrant birds, or speak of bodiless spirits that floated along the air like smoke, screaming from the winter gales but gently murmuring in the breezes of spring and summer.

For some reason that I cannot explain, these legends and folk-tales not only filled my mind with eerie fancies but made me think of one who was quite human and real. I began to wonder about Yasma—where was she now? What part was she taking in the celebration? And as my thoughts turned to her, an irrational fear crept into my mind—what if, like the maidens described in the poems, she had taken wing? Smiling at my own imaginings, I arose quietly from my couch of grass, and slowly and cautiously began to move about the edge of the crowd, while scanning the nearer forms and faces. In the pale light I could scarcely be distinguished from a native; and, being careful to keep to the shadows, I was apparently not noticed. And I had almost circled the clearing before I had any reason to pause.

All this time I had seen no sign of Yasma. I had almost given up hope of finding her when my attention was attracted to a solitary little figure hunched against a cabin wall in the dimness at the edge of the clearing. Even in the near-dark I could not fail to recognize her; and, heedless of the dancers surging and eddying through the open spaces, I made toward her in a straight line.

I will admit that I had some idea of the unwisdom of speaking to her tonight; but my impatience had gotten the better of my tongue.

"I am glad to see you here," I began, without the formality of a greeting. "You are not taking part in the dance, Yasma."

Yasma gave a start, and looked at me like one just awakened from deep sleep. At first her eyes showed no recognition; then it struck me there was just a spark of anger and even of hostility in her gaze.

"No, I am not taking part in the dance," she responded, listlessly. And then, after an interval, while I stood above her in embarrassed silence, "But why come to me now?... Why disturb me tonight of all nights?"

"I do not want to disturb you, Yasma," I apologized. "I just happened to see you here, and thought—"

My sentence was never finished. Suddenly I became aware that there was only vacancy where Yasma had been. And dimly I was conscious of a shadow-form slipping from me into the multitude of shadows.

In vain I attempted to follow her. She had vanished as completely as though she had been one of the ghostly women of the poems. No more that evening did I see her small graceful shape; but all the rest of the night, until the bonfire had smoldered to red embers and the crowd had dispersed, I wandered about disconsolately, myself like a ghost as I furtively surveyed the dancing figures. A deep, sinking uneasiness obsessed me; and my dejection darkened into despair as it became plainer that my quest was unavailing, and that Yasma had really turned against me.

CHAPTER IX
IN THE REDDENING WOODS

During the weeks before the firelight celebration, I had gradually made friends with the various natives. This was not difficult, for the people were as curious regarding me as I would have been regarding a Martian. At the same time, they were kindly disposed, and would never hesitate to do me any little favor, such as to help me in laying up my winter's supplies, or to advise me how to make a coat of goat's hide, or to tell me where the rarest herbs and berries were to be found, or to bring me liberal portions of any choice viand they chanced to be preparing.

I was particularly interested in Yasma's brothers and sisters, all of whom I met in quick succession. They were all older than she, and all had something of her naïvety and vivaciousness without her own peculiar charm. Her three sisters had found husbands among the men of the tribe, and two were already the mothers of vigorous toddling little sons and daughters; while her brothers, Karem and Barkodu, were tall, proud, and dignified of demeanor like their father.

With Karem, the elder, I struck up a friendship that was to prove my closest masculine attachment in Sobul. I well remember our first meeting; it was just after my convalescence from my long illness. One morning, in defiance of Yasma's warning, I had slipped off by myself into the woods, intending to go but a few hundred yards. But the joyous green of the foliage, the chirruping birds and the warm crystalline air had misled me; and, happy merely to be alive and free, I wandered on and on, scarcely noticing how I was overtaxing my strength. Then suddenly I became aware of an overwhelming faintness; all things swam around me; and I sank down upon a boulder, near to losing consciousness.... After a moment, I attempted to rise; but the effort was too much; I have a recollection of staggering like a drunken man, or reeling, of pitching toward the rocks....

Happily, I did not complete my fall. Saving me from the shattering stones, two strong arms clutched me about the shoulders, and wrenched me back to a standing posture.

In a daze, I looked up ... aware of the red and blue costume of a tribesman of Sobul ... aware of the two large black eyes that peered down at me half in amusement, half in sympathy. Those eyes were but the most striking features of a striking countenance; I remembered having already seen that high, rounded forehead, that long, slender, swarthy face with the aquiline nose, that untrimmed luxuriant full black beard.

"Come, come, I do not like your way of walking," the man declared, with a smile. And seeing that I was still too weak to reply, he continued, cheerfully, with a gesture toward a thicket to our rear, "If I had not been there gathering berries, this day might have ended sadly for you. Shall I not take you home?"

Leaning heavily upon him while with the gentlest care he led me along the trail, I found my way slowly back to the village.

And thus I made the acquaintance of Karem, brother of Yasma. At the time I did not know of the relationship; but between Karem and myself a friendship quickly developed. Even as he wound with me along the woodland track to the village, I felt strangely drawn toward this genial, self-possessed man; and possibly he felt a reciprocal attraction, for he came often thereafter to inquire how I was doing; and occasionally we had long talks, as intimate as my foreign birth and my knowledge of Pushtu would permit. I found him not at all unintelligent, and the possessor of knowledge that his sophisticated brothers might have envied. He told me more than I had ever known before about the habits of wood creatures, of wolves and squirrels, jackals, snakes and bears; he could describe where each species of birds had their nests, and the size and color of the eggs; he instructed me in the lore of bees, ants and beetles, and in the ways of the fishes in the swift-flowing streams. Later, when I had recovered my strength, he would accompany me on day-long climbs among the mountains, showing me the best trails and the easiest ascents—and so supplying me with knowledge that was to prove most valuable in time to come.

It was to Karem that I turned for an answer to the riddles of Sobul after Yasma had failed me. But in this respect he was not very helpful. He would smile indulgently whenever I hinted that I suspected a mystery; and would make some jovial reply, as if seeking to brush the matter aside with a gesture. This was especially the case on the day after the firelight festivities, when we went on a fishing expedition to a little lake on the further side of the valley. Although in a rare good humor, he was cleverly evasive when I asked anything of importance. What had been the purpose of the celebration? It was simply an annual ceremony held by his people, the ceremony of the autumn season. Why had Hamul-Kammesh attached so much significance to the flight of the birds? That was mere poetic symbolism; the birds had been taken as typical of the time of year. Then what reason for the excitement of the people?—and what had Yulada to do with the affair? Of course, Yulada had nothing to do with it at all; but the people thought she had ordered the ceremonies, and they had been swayed by a religious mania, which Hamul-Kammesh, after the manner of soothsayers, had encouraged for the sake of his own influence.

Such were Karem's common-sense explanations. On the surface they were convincing; and yet, somehow, I was not convinced. For the moment I would be persuaded; but thinking over the facts at my leisure, I would feel sure that Karem had left much unstated.

My dissatisfaction with his replies was most acute when I touched upon the matter closest to my heart. I described Yasma's conduct during the celebration; confided how surprised I had been, and how pained; and confessed my fear that I had committed the unpardonable sin by intruding during an important rite.

To all that I said Karem listened with an attentive smile.

"Why, Prescott," he returned (I had taught him to call me by my last name), "you surprise me! Come, come, do not be so serious! Who can account for a woman's whims? Certainly, not I! When you are married like me, and have little tots running about your house ready to crawl up your knee whenever you come in, you'll know better than to try to explain what the gods never intended to be explained by any man!" And Karem burst into laughter, and slapped me on the back good-naturedly, as though thus to dispose of the matter.

However, I was not to be sidetracked so easily. I did not join in Karem's laughter; I even felt a little angry. "But this wasn't just an ordinary whim," I argued. "There was something deeper in it. There was some reason I don't understand, and can't get at no matter how I try."

"Then why not save trouble, and quit trying?" suggested Karem, still good-natured despite my sullenness. "Come, it's a splendid day; let's enjoy it while we can!"

And he pointed ahead to a thin patch of blue, vaguely visible through a break in the trees. "See, there's the lake already! I expect fishing will be good today!"

If I had required further proof that my wits had surrendered to Yasma's charms, I might have found evidence enough during the days that followed the tribal celebration. Though smarting from her avoidance of me, I desired nothing more fervently than to be with her again; and I passed half my waking hours in vainly searching for her. Day after day I would inquire for her at her father's cabin, would haunt the paths to the dwelling, would search the fields and vineyards in the hope of surprising her. Where had she gone, she who had always come running to greet me? Had she flown south like the wild birds? At this fancy I could only smile; yet always, with a lover's irrational broodings, I was obsessed by the fear that she was gone never to return. This dread might have risen to terror had the villagers not always been bringing me tidings of her: either they had just spoken with her, or had seen someone who had just spoken with her, or had observed her tripping by toward the meadows. Yet she was still elusive as though able to make herself invisible.

Nevertheless, after about a week my vigilance was rewarded. Stepping out into the chill gray of a mid-October dawn, I saw a slender little figure slipping along the edge of the village and across the fields toward the woods. My heart gave a great thump; without hesitation, I started in pursuit, not daring to call out lest I arouse the village, but determined not to lose sight of that slim flitting form. She did not glance behind, and could not have known that I was following, yet for some reason quickened her pace, so that I had to make an effort to match her speed.

Once out of earshot of the village, I paused to regain my breath, then at the top of my voice shouted, "Yasma! Yasma!"

Could it be that she had not heard me? On and on she continued, straight toward the dark fringe of the woods.

Dismayed and incredulous, I repeated my call, using my hands as a megaphone. This time it seemed to me that she halted momentarily; but she did not look back; and her pause could not have filled the space between two heart beats. In amazement, I observed her almost racing toward the woods!

But if she could run, so could I! With rising anger, yet scarcely crediting the report of my eyes, I started across the fields at a sprint. In a moment I should overtake Yasma—and then what excuse would she have to offer?

But ill fortune was still with me. In my heedless haste I stumbled over a large stone; and when, bruised and confused, I arose to my feet with an oath, it was to behold a slender form disappearing beyond the shadowy forest margin.

Although sure that I had again lost track of her, I continued the pursuit in a sort of dogged rage. There was but one narrow trail amid the densely matted undergrowth; and along this trail I dashed, encouraged by the sight of small fresh-made footprints amid the damp earth. But the maker of those footprints must have been in a great hurry, for although I pressed on until my breath came hard and my forehead was moist with perspiration, I could catch no glimpse of her, nor even hear any stirring or rustling ahead.

At length I had lost all trace of her. The minute footprints came to an end, as though their creator had vanished bird-like; and I stood in bewilderment in the mournful twilight of the forest, gazing up at the lugubrious green of pine and juniper and at the long twisted branches of oak and ash and wild peach, red-flecked and yellow and already half leafless.

How long I remained standing there I do not know. It was useless to go on, equally useless to retrace my footsteps. The minutes went by, and nothing happened. A bird chirped and twittered from some unseen twig above; a squirrel came rustling toward me, and with big frightened eyes hopped to the further side of a tree-trunk; now and then an insect buzzed past, with a dismal drone that seemed the epitome of all woe. But that was all—and of Yasma there was still no sign.

Then, when I thought of her and remembered her loveliness, and how she had been my playmate and comrade, I was overcome with the sorrow of losing her, and a teardrop dampened my cheek, and I heaved a long-drawn sigh.

And as if in response to that sigh, the bushes began to shake and quiver. And a sob broke the stillness of the forest, and I was as if transfixed by the sound of a familiar voice.

And out of the tangle of weeds and shrubs a slender figure arose, with shoulders heaving spasmodically; and with a cry I started forward and received into my arms the shuddering, speechless, clinging form of Yasma.

It was minutes before either of us could talk. Meanwhile I held the weeping girl closely to me, soothing her as I might have done a child. So natural did this seem that I quite forgot the strangeness of the situation. My mind was filled with sympathy, sympathy for her distress, and wonder at her odd ways; and I had no desire except to comfort her.

"Tell me just what has happened, Yasma," I said, when her sobbing had died down to a rhythmic murmuring. "What has happened—to make you so sad?"

To my surprise, she broke away, and stood staring at me at arm's length. Her eyes were moist with an inexpressible melancholy; there was something so pitiful about her that I could have taken her back into my arms forthwith.

"Oh, my friend," she cried, with a vehemence I could not understand, "why do you waste time over me? Have nothing to do with me! I am not worth it!" And she turned as if to flee again into the forest; but I seized her hand and drew her slowly back to me.

"Yasma! Yasma!" I remonstrated, peering down into those wistful brown eyes that burned with some dark-smoldering fire. "What has made you behave so queerly? Tell me, do you no longer care for me? Do you not—do you not love me?"

At these words, the graceful head sagged low upon the quivering shoulders. A crimson flush mounted the slender neck, and suffused the soft, well rounded cheeks; the averted eyes told the story they were meant to conceal.

Then, without further hesitation, my arms closed once more about her. And again she clung close, this time not with the unconscious eagerness of a child craving protection, but with all the fury and force of her impetuous nature.

A few minutes later, a surprising change had come over her. We had left the woods, and she was sitting at my side in a little glade by a brooklet. The tears had been dried from her eyes, which were still red and swollen; but in her face there was a happy glow, and I thought she had never looked quite so beautiful before.

For a while we sat gazing in silence at the tattered and yet majestic line of the forest, a phantom pageant whose draperies of russet and cinnamon and fiery crimson and dusty gold were lovely almost beyond belief. A strange enchantment had come over us; and we were reluctant to break the charm.

Yet there were questions that kept stirring in my mind; questions to which finally I was forced to give words.

"Tell me, Yasma," I asked, suddenly, "why have you been behaving so queerly? Why were you running away from me? Is there something about me that frightened you?"

It was as if my words had brought back the evil spell. Her features contracted into a frown; the darkness returned to her eyes, which again burned with some unspoken sorrow; a look of fear, almost like that of a haunted creature, flitted across her face.

"Oh, you must never ask that!" she protested, in such dismay that I pitied her even while I wondered. "You must never ask—never, never!"

"Why not?" I questioned. "What mystery can there be to hide?"

"There is no mystery," she declared. And then, with quick inconsistency, "But even if there were, you should not ask!"

"But why?" I demanded. "Now, Yasma, you mustn't treat me like a five-year-old. What have I done to offend you? Tell me, what have I done?"

"It is nothing that you have done," she mumbled, avoiding my gaze.

"Then is it something someone else has done? Come, let me know just what is wrong!"

"I cannot tell you! I cannot!" she cried, with passion. And, rising abruptly and turning to me with eyes aflame, "Oh, why must you insist on knowing? Haven't I done everything to protect you from knowing? Do you think it has been easy—easy for me to treat you like this? But it is wrong to love you! wrong even to encourage you! Only evil can come of it! Oh, why did you ever, ever have to come among our tribe?"

Having delivered herself of this outburst, Yasma paced back and forth, back and forth amid the dense grass, with fists clenched and head upraised to the heavens, like one in an extremity of distress.

But I quickly arose and went to her, and in a moment she was again in my arms.

Truly, as Karem had declared, the ways of women are not to be explained! But I felt that there was more meaning than I had discovered in her behavior; I was sure that she had not acted altogether without reason, and, remembering all that had puzzled me, I was determined to probe if possible to the roots of her seeming caprice.

"You have never been the same to me since the firelight celebration," I said, when her emotion had spent itself and we once more sat quietly side by side in the grass. "Maybe something happened then to make you despise me."

"No, not to make me despise you!" she denied, emphatically. "It was not your fault at all!"

"Then what was it?" I urged.

"Nothing. Only that Hamul—Hamul—"

In manifest confusion, she checked herself.

"Hamul-Kammesh?" I finished for her, convinced that here was a clue.

But she refused to answer me or to mention the soothsayer again; and, lest the too-ready tears flow once more, I had to abandon the topic. None the less, I had not forgotten her references to Hamul-Kammesh and his prophecies.

But I still attached no importance to the predictions—was I to be dismayed by mere superstition? I was conscious only that I felt an overwhelming tenderness toward Yasma, and that she was supremely adorable; and it seemed to me that her love was the sole thing that mattered. At her first kiss, my reason had abdicated; I was agitated no longer by scruples, doubts or hesitancies; my former objects in life appeared pallid and dull by contrast with this warm, breathing, emotional girl. For her sake I would have forsworn my chosen work, forsworn the friends I had known, forsworn name and country—yes, even doomed myself to lasting exile in this green, world-excluding valley!

In as few words as possible I explained the nature of my feelings. I was able to give but pale expression to the radiance of my emotions; but I am sure that she understood. "I do not know what it is that holds you from me, Yasma," I finished. "Surely, you realize that you are dearer to me than my own breath. You made me very happy a little while ago when you came into my arms—why not make me happy for life? You could live with me here in a cabin in Sobul, or maybe I could take you with me to see the world I come from, and you would then know where the clouds go, and see strange cities with houses as tall as precipices and people many as the leaves of a tree. What do you say, Yasma? Don't you want to make us both happy?"

Yasma stared at me with wide-lidded eyes in which I seemed to read infinite longing.

"You know I would!" she cried. "You know I would—if I could! But ours is a strange people, and our ways are not your ways. There is so much you do not understand, so much which even I do not understand! It all makes me afraid, oh, terribly afraid!"

"Do not be afraid, Yasma dear," I murmured, slipping my arm about her shoulders. "I will protect you."

"You cannot protect me!" she lamented, withdrawing. "You cannot even protect yourself! There is so much, so much from which none can protect themselves!"

Not realizing what she meant, I let this warning slip past.

"All that I know," I swore, passionately, "is that I want you with me—want you with me always! Let happen what may, I want you—and have never wanted anything so much before!"

"Oh, do not speak of that now!" she burst forth, in a tone almost of command. "Do not speak of that now! First there are things you must know—things I cannot explain!" And she sat with eyes averted, gazing toward the scarlet and vermilion dishevelled trees, whose branches waved like ghostly danger signals in the rising wind.

"What things must I know?"

"You will have to wait and find out. Maybe, like us, you will feel them without being told; but maybe time alone will be your teacher. The traditions of my tribe would stop me from telling you even if I knew how. But do not be surprised if you learn some very, very strange things."

"Strange or not strange," I vowed, "all I know is that I love you. All I care to learn is when—when, Yasma, you will say to me—"

"Not until the spring," she murmured, with such finality that I felt intuitively the uselessness of argument. "Not until the flowers come out from their winter hiding, and the birds fly north. Then you will know more about our tribe."

Without further explanation, she sprang impulsively from her seat of grass. "Come," she warned me, pointing to a gray mass that was obscuring the northern peaks. "Come, a storm is on the way! If we don't hurry, we'll be wet through and through!"

And she flitted before me toward the village with such speed that I could scarcely get another word with her.

CHAPTER X
THE IBANDRU TAKE WING

As October drifted by and November loomed within two weeks' beckoning, a striking change came over Sobul. The very elements seemed to feel and to solemnize that change, which was as much in the spirit of things as in their physical aspect; and the slow-dying autumn seemed stricken with a bitter foretaste of winter. Cold winds began to blow, and even in the seclusion of the valley they shrieked and wailed with demonic fury; torn and scattered clouds scudded like great shadows over granite skies, and occasionally gave token of their ill will in frantic outbursts of rain; ominous new white patches were forming about the peaks, to vanish within a few hours, and appear again and vanish once more; and daily the dead leaves came drifting down in swarms and showers of withered brown and saffron and mottled red, while daily the flocks of winged adventurers went darting and screeching overhead on their way beyond the mountains.

But the stormy days, with all the wildness and force and passionate abandon of wind and rain, were less impressive for me than the days of calm. Then, when the placid sky shone in unbroken blue, all nature seemed sad with a melancholy I had never felt among my native hills. There was something tragic about the tranquil, ragged forest vistas, shot through as with an inner light of deep golden and red, and standing bared in mute resignation to the stroke of doom. But there was something more than tragic; there was something spectral about those long waiting lines of trees, with their foliage that at times appeared to reflect the sunset, and at times seemed like the painted tapestries of some colossal dream pageant. More and more, as I gazed in a charmed revery at the gaudy death-apparel of the woods, I was obsessed with the sense of some immanent presence, some weird presence that hovered intangibly behind the smoldering autumn fires, some presence that I could not think of without a shudder and that filled me with an unreasonable awe.

Certainly my feelings, uncanny as they were, were to be justified only too fully by time. Already I had more than a suspicion that the season of southward-flying birds was a season of mystic meaning for the Ibandru, but little did I understand just how important it was. Only by degrees did realization force itself upon me; and then I could only gape, and rub my eyes, and ask if I were dreaming. Stranger than any tale I had ever read in the Arabian Nights, stranger than any fancy my fevered mind had ever beckoned forth, was the reality that set the Ibandru apart from all other peoples on earth.

As the weeks went by, the agitation I had noted among the natives was intensified rather than lessened. I was aware of a sense of waiting which grew until the very atmosphere seemed anxious and strained; and I observed that the men and women no longer went as usual about their tasks, but flitted to and fro aimlessly or nervously or excitedly, as though they had no definite place in the world and were hesitating on the brink of some fearful decision.

And then, one day when October was a little beyond mid-career, I thought I detected another change. At first I was not sure, and accused my imagination of playing pranks; but it was not long before I ceased to have any doubts. The population of Sobul was dwindling! Not half so many children as before were romping in the open among the houses, not half so many women could be seen bustling about the village, or so many men roaming the fields—the entire place wore a sudden air of desolation. And in more than one cabin, previously the home of a riotous family, the doors swung no longer upon their wooden hinges, but through the open window-places I caught glimpses of bare floors and dark walls innocent of human occupancy.

When had the people gone? And where? I had not seen anyone leave, nor been told that anyone was to leave; and I witnessed no ceremonies of farewell. Could the missing ones be victims of some terror that came down "like a wolf on the fold" and snatched them away in the night? Or were they merely visiting some other tribe in some other secluded valley?

These problems puzzled me incessantly; but when I turned to the Ibandru for information, their answers were tantalizing. They did not deny that some of their tribesmen had left, and did not claim that this had been unexpected or mystifying; but they were either unable or unwilling to furnish any details; and I was not sure whether they felt that I was probing impertinently into their affairs, or whether some tribal or religious mandate sealed their lips.

I particularly remember the answers of Karem and Yasma. The former, with his usual jovial way of avoiding the issue, advised me to have no worries; the whole matter was really no concern of mine, and I might be assured that the missing ones were not badly off or unhappy. By this time I must have learned that the Ibandru had queer ways, and I must prepare for things queerer still; but, until I was one with the tribe at heart, I must not expect to understand.

Yasma's answer, though vague enough, was more definite.

"Our absent friends," she said, while by turns a sad and an exalted light played across her mobile features, "have gone the way of the birds that fly south. Yulada has beckoned them, and they have escaped the winter's loneliness and cold, and have hastened where the bright flowers are, and the butterflies and bees. See!"—Ecstatically she pointed to a triangle of swift-moving dots that glided far above through the cloudless blue.—"They are like the wild geese! They flee from the biting gales and the frost, and will not return till the warm days are here again and the leaves come back to the trees. We must all go like them—all of us, all, all!"

"And I too—must I go?" I asked, never thinking of taking her words literally.

Yasma hesitated. The light faded from her eyes; an expression of sorrow, almost of compassion, flooded her face.

"That I cannot say," she returned, sadly. "You must feel the call within you, feel it as the birds do, drawing you on to lands where robins sing and the lilac blooms. No one can tell you how to feel it; it must come from within or not at all, and you yourself must recognize it. But oh, you cannot help recognizing it! It is so strong, so very strong!—and it takes your whole body and soul with it, draws you like a rainbow or a beautiful sunset; and bears you along as the wind bears a dead leaf. You cannot resist it any more than you can resist a terrible hunger—you must submit, or it will hurl you under!"

"I do not understand," said I, for despite the ardor of her words, I had only the dimmest idea of the overmastering force she described.

"Perhaps," she returned, gently, "you cannot know. You may be like a color-blind man trying to understand color. But oh, I hope not! I hope—ever and ever so much—that you'll hear the call thundering within you. Otherwise, you'll have to stay here by yourself the whole winter, while the snow falls and the wolves howl, and you won't see us again till spring!"

Her emotion seemed to be overcoming her. Fiercely she wiped a tear from her cheek; then turned from me, to give way to her misgivings in the seclusion of her father's cabin.

But I was not without my own misgivings. Her words had revived haunting premonitions; it was as if some sinister shadow hovered over me, all the more dread because formless. What unhallowed people were these Ibandru, to go slinking away like specters in the night? Were they a tribe of outlaws or brigands, hiding from justice in these impenetrable fastnesses? Or were they the sole survivors of some ancient race, endowed with qualities not given to ordinary humans? With new interest I recalled the stories told me by the Afghan guides before my fateful adventure: the reports that the Ibandru were a race of devils, winged like birds and with the power of making themselves invisible. Absurd as this tale appeared, might there not be the ghost of an excuse for it?

As for Yasma's predictions and warnings—what meaning had there been in them? Was it indeed possible that I might be left alone all winter in this desolate place? And was that why Abthar had advised me to make ready for the cold season while his own people had apparently done nothing to prepare? But, even so, how could they escape the winter? Was it not a mere poetic vagary to say, as Yasma had done, that they went to lands where robins sang and the lilac bloomed—how cross the interminable mountain reaches to the semi-torrid valleys of India or the warm Arabian plains? Or was it that, like the bears, they hibernated in caves? Or, like the wild geese that they watched so excitedly, were they swayed by some old migratory instinct, some impulse dormant or dead in most men but preserved for them by a long succession of nomad ancestors? Although reason scoffed at the idea, I had visions of them trekking each autumn across four or five hundred miles of wilderness to the borders of the Arabian Sea, surviving on provisions they had secreted along the route, and returning with the spring to their homes in Sobul.

Unlikely as this explanation appeared, nothing more plausible occurred to me. But as the days went by, my sense of mystery increased. The people were fleeing almost as though Sobul were plague-ridden—of that there could be no further doubt! Daily now I missed some familiar face; first a child who had come to me of evenings to run gay races in the fields; then an old woman who had sat each morning in the sun before her cabin; then Yasma's brother, Barkodu, whose tall sturdy form I had frequently observed in the village. And then one evening when I inquired for Karem, I was told that he was not to be seen; and the people's peculiar reserved expression testified that he had gone "the way of the birds that fly south." And, a day later, when I wished to see Abthar in the hope that he would relieve my perplexed mind, I found no one in the cabin except Yasma; and she murmured that her father would not be back till spring.

But did I make no effort to solve the enigma? Did I not strive to find out for myself where the absent ones had gone? Yes! I made many attempts—and with bewildering results. Even today I shudder to think of the ordeal I underwent; the remembrance of eerie midnights and strange shadows that flickered and vanished comes back to me after these many, many months; I feel again the cool, forest-scented breeze upon my nostrils as I crouch among the deep weeds at the village edge, or as I glide phantom-like beneath the trees in the cold starlight. For it was mainly at night that I wrestled with the Unknown; and it was at night that I received the most persuasive and soul-disturbing proof of the weirdness of the ways of Sobul.

My plans may not have been well laid, but they were the best I could conceive. From the fact that I had never seen any of the Ibandru leaving, and that more than once in the morning I had missed some face that had greeted me twelve hours before, I concluded that the people invariably fled by night. Acting on this view, I hid one evening in a clump of bushes on the outskirts of the village, resolved to wait if need be until dawn. True, no one might choose tonight for the migration; but in that case I should lie in hiding tomorrow night, and if necessary again on the night after.

As I lay sprawled among the bushes, whose dry leaves and twigs pricked and irritated my skin, I was prey to countless vexations. The night was cold, and I shivered as the wind cut through my thin garments; the night was long, and I almost groaned with impatience while the slow constellations crawled across the heavens; the night was dark, and fantastic fears flitted through my mind as I gazed through the gloom toward the ghostly line of the trees and cabins. Every now and then, when some wild creature called out querulously from the woods, I was swept by desire to flee; and more than once some harmless small beast, rustling a few yards off, startled me to alarm. But in the village nothing stirred, and the aloof, shadowy huts, scattered here and there like the monsters of a nightmare, seemed to bristle with unspeakable menace.

Yet nothing menacing became visible as the long reaches of the night dragged by and the constellations still swung monotonously between the faint black line of the eastern ranges and the equally faint black peaks to the west. At length, lulled by the sameness and the silence, I must have forgotten myself, must have drowsed a bit, for I have a recollection of coming to myself with a start, bewildered and with half clouded senses.... The night was as tranquil as before, the trees and houses as dark; but as I glanced skyward I detected the merest touch of gray. And, at the same time, I had a singular sense that I was no longer alone. Intently I gazed into the gloom—still nothing visible. But all the while that same shuddery feeling persisted, as if unseen eyes were watching me, unseen ears listening to my every motion. Again I felt an impulse to flee; my limbs quivered; my heart pounded; instinctively I crawled deeper into the bushes. And, as I did so, I saw that which made me catch my breath in horror.

From behind one of the nearer cabins, two long lithe shadows darted, gliding noiselessly toward me through the darkness. No ghost could have shown dimmer outlines, or walked on more silent feet, or flooded my whole being with more uncanny sensations. Straight toward me they strode, looming gigantic in my tortured imagination; and as they approached I hugged the bushes more closely, trembling lest the phantoms discover me. Then suddenly they swerved aside, and passed at a dozen paces; and through the stillness of the night came the dull rhythm of sandalled feet.

For a minute I watched in silence. Then, encouraged by the pale radiance which was swallowing the feebler stars and softening the blackness above, I choked down my fears and crept stealthily out of the thicket. Before me the two shadows were still vaguely visible, gliding rapidly toward the southern woods. Like a detective trailing his prey, I stumbled among the weeds and rocks in their wake. But, all the time, I felt that I was pursuing mere wraiths; and, though I walked my swiftest, I found it impossible to gain upon them. They were several hundred yards ahead, and several hundred yards ahead they remained, while I put forth my utmost effort and they appeared to make no effort at all. And at last, to my dismay, they reached the shaggy boundary of the woods; merged with it; and were blotted out.

With what poor patience I could still command, I took the only possible course. While dawn lent gradual color to the skies, I hovered at the forest edge; and in the first dismal twilight I began to inspect the ground, hopeful of discovering some telltale evidence.

But no evidence was to be had. I did indeed find the footprints I was looking for; the trouble was that I found too many footprints. Not two persons but twenty had passed on this path, which I recognized as a trail leading toward Yulada. But all the tracks were new-made, and all equally obscured by the others; and it was impossible to say which were the freshest, or to follow any in particular.

When I returned to the village, not a person was stirring among the cabins; an unearthly stillness brooded over the place, and I could have imagined it to be a town of the dead. Had I not been utterly fatigued by my night in the open, I might have been struck even more strongly by the solitude, and have paused to investigate; as it was, I made straight for my own hut, flung myself down upon my straw couch, and sank into a sleep from which I did not awaken until well past noon.

After a confused and hideous dream, in which I lay chained to a glacier while an arctic wind blew through my garments, I opened my eyes with the impression that the nightmare had been real. A powerful wind *was* blowing! I could hear it blustering and wailing among the treetops; through my open window it flickered and sallied with a breath that seemed straight from the Pole. Leaping to my feet, I hastily closed the great shutters I had constructed of pine wood; and, at the same time, I caught glimpses of gray skies with a scudding rack of clouds, and of little white flakes driving and reeling down.

In my surprise at this change in the weather, I was struck by premonitions as bleak as the bleak heavens. What of Yasma? How would she behave in the storm?—she who was apparently unprepared for the winter! Though I tried to convince myself that there was no cause for concern, an unreasoning something within me insisted that there was cause indeed. It was not a minute, therefore, before I was slipping on my goatskin coat.

But I might have spared my pains. At this instant there came a tapping from outside, and my heart began to beat fiercely as I shouted, "Come in!"

The log door moved upon its hinges, and a short slim figure slipped inside.

"Yasma!" I cried, surprised and delighted, as I forced the door shut in the face of the blast. But my surprise was swiftly to grow, and my delight to die; at sight of her wild, sad eyes, I started back in wonder and dismay. In part they burned with a mute resignation, and in part with the unutterable pain of one bereaved; yet at the same time her face was brightened with an indefinable exultation, as though beneath that vivid countenance some secret ecstasy glowed and smoldered.

"I have come to say good-bye," she murmured, in dreary tones. "I have come to say good-bye."

"Good-bye!"—It was as though I had heard that word long ago in a bitter dream. Yet how could I accept the decree? Passion took fire within me as I seized Yasma and pressed her to me.

"Do not leave me!" I pleaded. "Oh, why must you go away? Where must you go? Tell me, Yasma, tell me! Why must I stay here alone the whole winter long? Why can't I go with you? Or why can't you stay with me? Stay here, Yasma! We could be so happy together, we two!"

Tears came into her eyes at this appeal.

"You make me sad, very sad," she sighed, as she freed herself from my embrace. "I do not want to leave you here alone—and yet, oh what else can I do? The cold days have come, and my people call me, and I must go where the flowers are. Oh, you don't know how gladly I'd have you come with us; but you don't understand the way, and can't find it, and I can't show it to you. So I must go now, I must go, I must! for soon the last bird will have flown south."

Again she held out her hands as for a friendly greeting, and again I took her into my arms, this time with all the desperation of impending loss, for I was filled with a sense of certainties against which it was useless to struggle, and felt as if by instinct that she would leave despite all I could do or say.

But I did not realize quite how near the moment was. Slipping from my clasp, she flitted to the door, forcing it slightly open, so that the moaning and howling of the gale became suddenly accentuated. "Until the spring!" she cried, in mournful tones that seemed in accord with the tumult of the elements. "Until the spring!"—And a smile of boundless yearning and compassion glimmered across her face. Then the door rattled to a close, and I stood alone in that chilly room.

Blindly, like one bereft of his senses, I plunged out of the cabin, regardless of the gale, regardless of the snow that came wheeling down in dizzy flurries. But Yasma was not to be seen. For a moment I stood staring into the storm; then time after time I called out her name, to be answered only by the wind that sneered and snorted its derision. And at length, warmed into furious action, I set out at a sprint for her cabin, racing along unconscious of the buffeting blast and the beaten snow that pricked and stung my face.

All in vain! Arriving at Yasma's home, I flung open the great pine door without ceremony—to be greeted by the emptiness within. For many minutes I waited; but Yasma did not come, and the tempest shrieked and chuckled more fiendishly than ever.

At last, when the early twilight was dimming the world, I threaded a path back along the whitening ground, and among cabins with roofs like winter. Not a living being greeted me; and through the wide-open windows of the huts I had glimpses of naked and untenanted logs.

II
BLOSSOM AND SEED

CHAPTER XI
THE PRISONER

When I staggered back to my cabin through the snow-storm in the November dusk, I could not realize the ghastliness of my misfortune. My mind seemed powerless before the bleak reality; it was not until I had re-entered the cabin that I began to look the terror in the face. Then, when I had slammed the door behind me and stood silently in that frigid place, all my dread and loneliness and foreboding became concentrated in one point of acute agony. The shadows deepening within that dingy hovel seemed living, evil things; the wind that hissed and screeched without, with brief lulls and swift crescendos of fury, was like a chorus of demons; and such desolation of spirit was upon me that I could have rushed out into the storm, and delivered myself up to its numbing, fatal embrace.

It was long before, conscious of the increasing chill and the coaly darkness, I went fumbling about the room to make a light. Fortunately, I still had a half-used box of matches, vestiges of the world I had lost; and with their aid, I contrived to light a little wax candle.

But as I watched the taper fitfully burning, with sputtering yellow rays that only half revealed the bare walls of the room and left eerie shadows to brood in the corners, I almost wished that I had remained in darkness. How well I remembered Yasma's teaching me to make the candle; to melt the wax; to pour it into a little wooden mould; to insert the wick in the still viscid mass! Could it be but a month ago when she had stood with me in this very room, so earnestly and yet so gaily giving me instructions? Say rather that it was years ago, eons ago!—what relation could there be between that happy self, which had laughed with Yasma, and this forlorn self, which stood here abandoned in the darkness and the cold?

And as I thought of Yasma, and gazed at her handiwork, the full sense of my wretchedness swept over me. Could she really be gone, mysteriously gone, past any effort of mine to bring her back? Was it possible that many a long bitter day and cold lonely night would pass before I could see her again? Or, for that matter, how did I know that she would ever return?—How attach any hope to her vague promises? What if she could not keep those promises? What if calamity should overtake her in her hiding place? She might be ill, she might be crippled, she might be dead, and I would not even know it!

While such thoughts blundered through my mind, I tried to keep occupied by kindling some dry branches and oak logs in the great open fireplace. But my broodings persisted, and would not be stilled even after a wavering golden illumination filled the cabin. Outside, the storm still moaned like a band of driven souls in pain; and the uncanny fancy came to me that lost spirits were speaking from the gale; that the spirits of the Ibandru wandered homelessly without, and that Yasma, even Yasma, might be among them! Old folk superstitions, tales of men converted into wraiths and of phantoms that appeared as men, forced themselves upon my imagination; and I found myself harboring—and, for the moment, almost crediting—notions as strange as ever disturbed the primitive soul. What if the Ibandru were not human after all? Or what if, human for half the year, they roamed the air ghost-like for the other half? Or was it that, like the Greek Persephone, they must spend six months in the sunlight and six months in some Plutonian cave?

Preposterous as such questions would formerly have seemed, they did not impress me as quite absurd as I sat alone on the straw-covered floor of my log cave, gazing into the flames that smacked their lean lips rabidly, and listening to the gale that rushed by with a torrential roaring. Like a child who fears to have strayed into a goblin's den, I was unnerved and unmercifully the prey of my own imagination; I could not keep down the thought that there was something weird about my hosts. Now, as rarely before during my exile, I was filled with an overpowering longing for home and friends, for familiar streets, and safe, well-known city haunts; and I could almost have wept at the impossibility of escape. Except for Yasma—Yasma, whose gentleness held me more firmly than iron chains—I would have prayed to leave this dreary wilderness and never return.

Finally, in exhaustion as much of the mind as of the body, I sank down upon my straw couch, covered myself with my goatskin coat, and temporarily lost track of the world and its vexations. But even in sleep I was not to enjoy peace; confused dreams trailed me through the night; and in one, less blurred than the others, I was again with Yasma, and felt her kiss upon my cheek, wonderfully sweet and compassionate, and heard her murmur that I must not be sad or impatient but must wait for her till the spring. But even as she spoke a dark form intruded between us, and sealed our lips, and forced her away until she was no more than a specter in the far distance. And as in terror I gazed at the dark stranger, I recognized something familiar about her; and with a cry of alarm, I awoke, for the pose and features were those of Yulada!

Hours must have passed while I slept; the fire had smoldered low, and only one red ember, gaping like a raw untended wound, cast its illumination across the cabin. But through chinks in the walls a faint gray light was filtering in, and I could no longer hear the wind clamoring.

An hour or two later I arose, swallowed a handful of dried herbs by way of breakfast, and forced open the cabin door. It was an altered world that greeted me; the clouds had rolled away, and the sky, barely tinged with the last fading pink and buff of dawn, was of a pale, unruffled blue. But a white sheet covered the ground, and mantled the roofs of the log huts, and wove fantastic patterns over the limbs of leafless bushes and trees. All things seemed new-made and beautiful, yet all were wintry and forlorn—and what a majestic sight were the encircling peaks! Their craggy shoulders, yesterday bare and gray and dotted with only an occasional patch of white, were clothed in immaculate snowy garments, reaching far heavenward from the upper belts of the pines, whose dark green seemed powdered with an indistinguishable spray.

But I tried to forget that terrible and hostile splendor; urged by a hope that gradually flickered and went out, I made a slow round of the village. At each cabin I paused, peering through the window or knocking at the unbolted door and entering; and at each cabin I sank an inch nearer despair. As yet, of course, I had had no proof that I was altogether abandoned—might there not still be some old man or woman, some winter-loving hunter or doughty watchman, who had been left behind until the tribe's return in the spring? But no man, woman or child stirred in the white spaces between the cabins; no man, woman or child greeted me in any of the huts.... All was bare as though untenanted for months; and here an empty earthen pan or kettle hanging on the wall, there a dozen unshelled nuts forgotten in a corner, yonder a half-burnt candle or a cracked water jug or discarded sandal, were the only tokens of recent human occupancy.

It was but natural that I should feel most forlorn upon entering Yasma's cabin. How mournfully I gazed at the walls her eyes had beheld a short twenty-four hours before! and at a few scattered trifles that had been hers! My attention was especially caught by a little pink wildflower, shaped like a primrose, which hung drooping in a waterless jar; and the odd fancy came to me that this was like Yasma herself. Tenderly, urged by a sentiment I hardly understood, I lifted the blossom from the jar, pressed it against my bosom, and fastened it securely there.

The outside world now seemed bright and genial enough. From above the eastern peaks the sun beamed generously upon the windless valley; and there was warmth in his rays as he put the snow to flight and sent little limpid streams rippling across the fields. But to me it scarcely mattered whether the sun shone or the gale dashed by. Now there was an irony in the sunlight, an irony I resented even as I should have resented the bluster of the storm. Yet, paradoxically, it was to sunlit nature that I turned for consolation, for what but the trees and streams and soaring heights could make me see with broader vision? Scornful of consequences, I plodded through the slushy ground to the woods; and roaming the wide solitudes, with the snow and the soggy brown leaves beneath and the almost denuded branches above, I came to look upon my problems with my first trace of courage.

"This too will pass," I told myself, using the words of one older and wiser than I. And I pictured a time when these woods would be here, and I would not; pictured even a nearer time when I should roam them with laughter on my lips. What after all were a few months of solitude amid this magnificent world?

In such a mood I began to warm my flagging spirits and to plan for the winter. I should have plenty to occupy me; there were still many cracks and crannies in my cabin wall, which I must fill with clay; there was still much wood to haul from the forest; there were heavy garments to make from the skins supplied by the natives; and there would be my food to prepare daily from my hoard in the cabin, and my water to be drawn from the stream that flowed to the rear of village. Besides, I might be able to go on long tours of exploration; I might amuse myself by examining the mountain strata, and possibly even make some notable geological observations; and I might sometime—the thought intruded itself slyly and insidiously—satisfy my curiosity by climbing to Yulada.

Emboldened by such thoughts, I roamed the woods for hours, and returned to my cabin determined to battle unflinchingly and to emerge triumphant.

It will be needless to dwell upon the days that followed. Although the moments crawled painfully, each week an epoch and each month an age, very little occurred that is worthy of record. Yet somehow I did manage to occupy the time—what other course had I, this side of suicide or madness? As in remembrance of a nightmare, I recall how sometimes I would toil all the daylight hours to make my cabin snug and secure; how at other times I would wander across the valley to the lake shown me by Karem, catching fish with an improvised line, even though I had first to break through the ice; how, again, I would idly follow the half-wild goat herds that browsed in remote corners of the valley; how I would roam the various trails until I had mapped them all in my mind, and had discovered the only outlet in the mountains about Sobul—a long, prodigiously deep, torrent-threaded ravine to the north, which opened into another deserted valley capped by desolate and serrated snowpeaks. The discovery of this valley served only to intensify my sense of captivity, for it brought me visions of mountain after mountain, range after range, bleak and unpopulated, which stretched away in frozen endless succession.

But the days when I could rove the mountains were days of comparative happiness. Too often the trails, blocked by the deep soft drifts or the ice-packs, were impassable for one so poorly equipped as I; and too often the blizzards raged. Besides, the daylight hours were but few, since the sun-excluding mountain masses made the dawn late and the evening early; and often the tedium seemed unendurable when I sat in my cabin at night, watching the flames that danced and crackled in the fireplace, and dreaming of Yasma and the spring, or of things still further away, and old friends and home. At times, scarcely able to bear the waiting, I would pace back and forth like a caged beast, back and forth, from the fire to the woodpile, and from the woodpile to the fire. At other times, more patient, I would amuse myself by trying to kindle some straw with bits of flint, or by returning to the ways of my boyhood and whittling sticks into all manner of grotesque designs. And occasionally, when the mood was upon me, I would strain my eyes by the flickering log blaze, confiding my diary to the notebook I had picked up in our old camp beyond the mountain. For the purposes of this diary, I had but one pencil, which gradually dwindled to a stub that I could hardly hold between two fingers—and with the end of the pencil, late in the winter, the diary also came to a close.

Although this record was written merely as a means of whiling away the hours and was not intended for other eyes, I find upon opening it again that it describes my plight more vividly than would be possible for me after the passage of years; and I am tempted to quote a typical memorandum.

As I peer at that curiously cramped and tortured handwriting, my eyes pause at the following:

"Monday, December 29th. Or it may be Tuesday the 30th, for I fear I have forgotten to mark one of the daily notches on the cabin walls, by which I keep track of the dates. All day I was forced to remain in my cabin, for the season's worst storm was raging. Only once did I leave shelter, and that was to get water. But the stream was frozen almost solid, and it was a task to pound my way through the ice with one of the crude native axes. Meanwhile the gale beat me in the face till my cheeks were raw; the snow came down in a mist of pellets that half blinded me; and a chill crept through my clothes till my very skin seemed bared to the ice-blast. I was fifteen minutes in thawing after I had crept back to the cabin. But even within the cabin there seemed no way to keep warm, for the wind rushed in through cracks that I could not quite fill; and the fire, though I heaped it with fuel, was feeble against the elemental fury outside.

"But the cold would be easier to bear than the loneliness. There is little to do, almost nothing to do; and I sit brooding on the cabin floor, or stand brooding near the fire; and life seems without aim or benefit. Strange thoughts keep creeping through my mind—visions of a limp form dangling on a rope from log rafters; or of a half-buried form that the snow has numbed to forgetfulness. But always there are other visions to chide and reproach; I remember a merry day in the woods, when two brown eyes laughed at me from beneath auburn curls; and I hear voices that call as if from the future, and see hands that take mine gently and restrain them from violence. Perhaps I am growing weak of mind and will, for my emotions flow like a child's; I would be ashamed to admit—though I confess it freely enough to the heedless paper—that more than once, in the long afternoon and the slow dismal twilight, the tears rolled down from my eyes.

"As I write these words, it is evening—only seven o'clock, my watch tells me, though I might believe it to be midnight. The blazes still flare in the fireplace, and I am stretched full-length on the floor, trying to see by the meager light. The storm has almost died down; only by fits and starts it mutters now, like a beast whose frenzy has spent itself. But other, more ominous sounds fill the air. From time to time I hear the barking of a jackal, now near, now far; while louder and more long-drawn and mournful, there comes at intervals the fierce deep wailing of a wolf, answered from the remote woods by other wolves, till all the world seems to resound with a demoniac chorus. Of all noises I have ever heard, this is to me the most terrorizing; and though safe within pine walls, I tremble where I lie by the fire, even as the cave-man may have done at that same soul-racking sound. I know, of course, how absurd this is; yet I have pictures of sly slinking feet that pad silently through the snow, and keen hairy muzzles that trail my footsteps even to this door, and long gleaming jaws that open. Only by forcing myself to write can I keep my mind from such thoughts; but, even so, I shudder whenever that dismal call comes howling, howling from the dark, as if with all the concentrated horror and ferocity in the universe!"

CHAPTER XII
THE MISTRESS OF THE PEAK

D uring the long months of solitude I let my gaze travel frequently toward the southern mountains and Yulada. Like the image of sardonic destiny, she still stood afar on the peak, aloof and imperturbable, beckoning and unexplained as always.... And again she drew me toward her with that inexplicable fascination which had been my undoing. As when I had first seen her from that other valley to the south, I felt a curious desire to mount to her, to stand at her feet, to inspect her closely and lay my hands upon her; and against that desire neither Yasma's warnings nor my own reason had any power. She was for me the unknown; she represented the mysterious, the alluring, the unattained, and all that was most youthful and alive within me responded to her call.

Yet Yulada was a discreet divinity, and did not offer herself too readily to the worshipper. Was it that she kept herself deliberately guarded, careful not to encourage the intruder? So I almost thought as I made attempt after attempt to reach her. It is true, of course, that I did not choose the most favorable season; likewise, it is true that I was exceedingly reckless, for solitary mountain climbing in winter is hardly a sport for the cautious. But, even so, I could not stamp out the suspicion that more than natural agencies were retarding me.

My first attempt occurred but a week after Yasma's departure. Most of the recent snow had melted from the mountain slopes, and the temperature was so mild that I foresaw no exceptional difficulties. I had just a qualm, I must admit, about breaking my word to Yasma—but had not the promise been extorted by unfair pleas? So, at least, I reasoned; and, having equipped myself with my goatskin coat, with a revolver and matches, and with food enough to last overnight if need be, I set out early one morning along one of the trails I had followed with Karem.

For two hours I advanced rapidly enough, reaching the valley's end and mounting along a winding path amid pine woods. The air was brisk and invigorating, the sky blue and clear; scarcely a breeze stirred, and scarcely a cloud drifted above. From time to time, through rifts in the foliage, I could catch glimpses of my goal, that gigantic steel-gray womanly form with hands everlastingly pointed toward the clouds and the stars. She seemed never to draw nearer, though my feet did not lag in the effort to reach her; but the day was still young, and I was confident that long before sunset I should meet her face to face.

Then suddenly my difficulties began. The trail became stonier and steeper, though that did not surprise me; the trail became narrower and occasionally blocked with snow, though that did not surprise me either; great boulders loomed in my way, and sometimes I had to crawl at the brink of a ravine, though that again I had expected. But the real obstacle was not anticipated. Turning a bend in the wooded trail, I was confronted with a sheer wall of rock, a granite mass broken at one end by a sort of natural stairway over which it seemed possible to climb precariously. I remembered how Karem and I had helped one another up this very ascent, which was by no means the most difficult on the mountain; but in the past month or two its aspect had changed alarmingly. A coating of something white and glistening covered the rock; in places the frosty crystals had the look of a frozen waterfall, and in places the icicles pointed downward in long shaggy rows.

Would it be possible to pass? I could not tell, but did not hesitate to try; and before long I had an answer. I had mounted only a few yards when my feet gave way, and I went sprawling backward down the rocky stair. How near I was to destruction I did not know; the first thing I realized was that I was clinging to the overhanging branch of a tree, while beneath me gaped an abyss that seemed bottomless.

A much frightened but a soberer man, I pulled myself into the tree, and climbed back to safety. As I regained the ground, I had a glimpse of Yulada standing silently far above, with a thin wisp of vapor across her face, as if to conceal the grim smile that may have played there. But I had seen enough of her for one day, and slowly and thoughtfully took my way back to the valley.

From that time forth, and during most of the winter, I had little opportunity for further assaults upon Yulada. If that thin coat of November ice had been enough to defeat me, what of the more stubborn ice of December and the deep drifts of January snow? Even had there not been prospects of freezing to death among the bare, wind-beaten crags, I should not have dared to entrust myself to the trails for fear of wolf-packs. Yet all winter Yulada stared impassively above, a mockery and a temptation—the only thing in human form that greeted me during those interminable months!

I shall pass over the eternities between my first attempt upon Yulada in November and my more resolute efforts in March. But I must not forget to describe my physical changes. I had grown a bushy brown beard, which hid my chin and upper lip and spread raggedly over my face; my hair hung as long and untended as a wild man's; while from unceasing exertions in the open, my limbs had developed a strength they had never known before, and I could perform tasks that would have seemed impossible a few months earlier.

Hence it was with confidence that I awaited the spring. Daily I scanned the mountains after the first sign of a thaw in the streams; I noted how streaks and furrows gradually appeared in the white of the higher slopes; how the gray rocky flanks began to protrude, first almost imperceptibly, then more boldly, as though casting off an unwelcome garb, until great mottled patches stood unbared to the sunlight. Toward the middle of March there came a week of unseasonably warm days, when the sun shone from a cloudless sky and a new softness was in the air. And then, when half the winter apparel of the peaks was disappearing as at a magic touch and the streams ran full to the brim and the lake overflowed, I decided to pay my long-postponed visit to Yulada.

Almost exultantly I set forth early one morning. The first stages of the climb could hardly have been easier; it was as though nature had prepared the way. The air was clear and stimulating, yet not too cool; and the comparative warmth had melted the last ice from the lower rocks. Exhilarated by the exercise, I mounted rapidly over slopes that would once have been a formidable barrier. Still Yulada loomed afar, with firm impassive face as always; but I no longer feared her, for surely, I thought, I should this day touch her with my own hands! As I strode up and up in the sunlight, I smiled to remember my old superstitions—what was Yulada after all but a rock, curiously shaped perhaps, but no more terrifying than any other rock!

Even when I had passed the timber-line, and strode around the blue-white glaciers at the brink of bare ravines, I still felt an unwonted bravado. Yulada was drawing nearer, noticeably nearer, her features clear-cut on the peak—and how could she resist my coming? In my self-confidence, I almost laughed aloud, almost laughed out a challenge to that mysterious figure, for certainly the few intervening miles could not halt me!

So, at least, I thought. But Yulada, if she were capable of thinking, must have held otherwise. Even had she been endowed with reason and with omnipotence, she could hardly have made a more terrible answer to my challenge. I was still plodding up the long, steep grades, still congratulating myself upon approaching success, when I began to notice a change in the atmosphere. It was not only that the air was growing sharper and colder, for that I had expected; it was that a wind was rising from the northwest, blowing over me with a wintry violence. In alarm, I glanced back—a stone-gray mass of clouds was sweeping over the northern mountains, already casting a shadow across the valley, and threatening to enwrap the entire heavens.

Too well I recognized the signs—only too well! With panicky speed, more than once risking a perilous fall, I plunged back over the path I had so joyously followed. The wind rose till it blew with an almost cyclonic fury; the clouds swarmed above me, angry and ragged-edged; Yulada was forgotten amid my dread visions of groping through a blizzard. Yet once, as I reached a turn in the trail, I caught a glimpse of her standing far above, her lower limbs overshadowed by the mists, her head obscured as though thus to mock my temerity.

And what if I did finally return to my cabin safely? Before I had regained the valley, the snow was whirling about me on the arms of the high wind, and the whitened earth, the chill air and the screeching gale had combined to accentuate my sense of defeat.

It might be thought that I would now renounce the quest. But there is in my nature some stubbornness that only feeds on opposition; and far from giving up, I watched impatiently till the storm subsided and the skies were washed blue once more; till the warmer days came and the new deposits of snow thawed on the mountain slopes. Two weeks after being routed by the elements, I was again on the trail to Yulada.

The sky was once more clear and calm; a touch of spring was in the air, and the sun was warmer than in months. Determined that no ordinary obstacle should balk me, I trudged with scarcely a pause along the winding trail; and, before many hours, I had mounted above the last fringe of the pines and deodars. At last I reached the point where I had had to turn back two weeks ago; at last I found myself nearer to the peak than ever before on all my solitary rambles, and saw the path leading ahead over bare slopes and around distorted crags toward the great steel-gray figure. The sweetness of triumph began to flood through my mind as I saw Yulada take on monstrous proportions, the proportions of a fair-sized hill; I was exultant as I glanced at the sky, and observed it to be still serene. There remained one more elevated saddle to be crossed, then an abrupt but not impossible grade of a few hundred yards—probably no more than half an hour's exertion, and Yulada and I should stand together on the peak!

But again the unexpected was to intervene. If I had assumed that no agency earthly or divine could now keep me from my goal, I had reckoned without my human frailties. It was a little thing that betrayed me, and yet a thing that seemed great enough. I had mounted the rocky saddle and was starting on a short descent before the final lap, when enthusiasm made me careless. Suddenly I felt myself slipping!

Fortunately, the fall was not a severe one; after sliding for a few yards over the stones, I was stopped with a jolt by a protruding rock.

Somewhat dazed, I started to arise ... when a sharp pain in my left ankle filled me with alarm. What if a tendon had been sprained? Among these lonely altitudes, that might be a calamity! But when I attempted to walk, I found my injury not quite so bad as I had feared. The ankle caused me much pain, yet was not wholly useless; so that I diagnosed the trouble as a simple strain rather than a sprain.

But there could be no further question of reaching Yulada that day. With a bitter glance at the disdainful, indomitable mistress of the peak, I started on my way back to Sobul. And I was exceedingly lucky to get back at all, for my ankle distressed me more and more as I plodded downward, and there were moments when it seemed as if it would not bear me another step.

So slowly did I move that I had to make camp that evening on the bare slopes at the edge of the forest; and it was not until late the following day that I re-entered the village. And all during the return trip, when I lay tossing in the glow of the campfire, or when I clung to the wall-like ledges in hazardous descents, I was obsessed by strange thoughts; and in my dreams that night I saw a huge taunting face, singularly like Yulada's, which mocked me that I should match my might against the mountain's.

CHAPTER XIII
THE BIRDS FLY NORTH

t was with a flaming expectation and a growing joy that I watched the spring gradually burst into blossom. The appearance of the first green grass, the unfolding of the pale yellowish leaves on the trees, the budding of the earliest wildflowers and the cloudy pink and white of the orchards, were as successive signals from a new world. And the clear bright skies, the fresh gentle breezes, and the birds twittering from unseen branches, all seemed to join in murmuring the same refrain: the warmer days were coming, the days of my deliverance! Soon, very soon, the Ibandru would be back! And among the Ibandru I should see Yasma!

Every morning now I awakened with reborn hope; and every morning, and all the day, I would go ambling about the village, peering into the deserted huts and glancing toward the woods for sign of some welcome returning figure. But at first all my waiting seemed of no avail. The Ibandru did not return; and in the evening I would slouch back to my cabin in dejection that would always make way for new hope. Day after day passed thus; and meantime the last traces of winter were vanishing, the fields became dotted with waving rose-red and violet and pale lemon tints; the deciduous trees were taking on a sturdier green; insects began to chirp and murmur in many a reviving chorus; and the woods seemed more thickly populated with winged singers.

And while I waited and still waited, insidious fears crept into my mind. Could it be that the Ibandru would not return at all?—that Yasma had vanished forever, like the enchanted princess of a fairy tale?

But after I had tormented myself to the utmost, a veil was suddenly lifted.

One clear day in mid-April I had strolled toward the woods, forgetting my sorrows in contemplating the green spectacle of the valley. Suddenly my attention was attracted by a swift-moving triangle of black dots, which came winging across the mountains from beyond Yulada, approaching with great speed and disappearing above the white-tipped opposite ranges. I do not know why, but these birds—the first I had observed flying north—filled me with an unreasonable hope; long after they were out of sight I stood staring at the blue sky into which they had faded, as though somehow it held the secret at which I clutched.

I was aroused from my reveries by the startled feeling that I was no longer alone. At first there was no clear reason for this impression; it was as though I had been informed by some vague super-sense. Awakened to reality, I peered into the thickets, peered up at the sky, scanned the trees and the earth alertly—but there was no sight or sound to confirm my suspicions. Minutes passed, and still I waited, expectant of some unusual event....

And then, while wonder kept pace with impatience, I thought I heard a faint rustling in the woods. I was not sure, but I listened intently.... Again the rustling, not quite so faint as before ... then a crackling as of broken twigs! Still I was not sure—perhaps it was but some tiny creature amid the underbrush. But, even as I doubted, there came the crunching of dead leaves trodden under; then the sound—unmistakably the sound—of human voices whispering!

My heart gave a thump; I was near to shouting in my exultation. Happy tears rolled down my cheeks; I had visions of Yasma returning, Yasma clasped once more in my arms—when I became aware of two dark eyes staring at me from amid the shrubbery.

"Karem!" I cried, and sprang forward to seize the hands of my friend.

Truly enough, it was Karem—Karem as I had last seen him, Karem in the same blue and red garments, somewhat thinner perhaps, but otherwise unchanged!

He greeted me with an emotion that seemed to match my own. "It is long, long since we have met!" was all he was able to say, as he shook both my hands warmly, while peering at me at arm's length.

Then forth from the bushes emerged a second figure, whom I recognized as Julab, another youth of the tribe. He too was effusive in his greetings; he too seemed delighted at our reunion.

But if I was no less delighted, it was not chiefly of the newcomers that I was thinking. One thought kept flashing through my mind, and I could not wait to give it expression. How about Yasma? Where was she now? When should I see her? Such questions I poured forth in a torrent, scarcely caring how my anxiety betrayed me.

"Yasma is safe," was Karem's terse reply. "You will see her before long, though just when I cannot say."

And that was the most definite reply I could wrench from him. Neither he nor Julab would discuss the reappearance of their people; they would not say where they had been, nor how far they had gone, nor how they had returned, nor what had happened during their absence. But they insisted on turning the conversation in my direction. They assured me how much relieved they were to find me alive and well; they questioned me eagerly as to how I had passed my time; they commented with zest upon my changed appearance, my ragged clothes and dense beard; and they ended by predicting that better days were in store.

More mystified than ever, I accompanied the two men to their cabins.

"We must make ready to till the fields," they reminded me, as we approached the village, "for when the trees again lose their leaves there will be another harvest." And they showed me where, unknown to me, spades and shovels and plows had been stored in waterproof vaults beneath the cabins; and they surprised me by pointing out the bins of wheat and sacks of nuts and dried fruits, preserved from last year's produce and harbored underground, so that when the people returned to Sobul they might have full rations until the ripening of the new crop.

Before the newcomers had been back an hour, they were both hard at work in the fields. I volunteered my assistance; and was glad to be able to wield a shovel or harrow after my long aimless months. The vigorous activity in the open air helped to calm my mind and to drive away my questionings; yet it could not drive them away wholly, and I do not know whether my thoughts were most on the soil I made ready for seeding or on things far-away and strange. Above all, I kept thinking of Yasma, kept remembering her in hope that alternated with dejection. Could it be true, as Karem had said, that I was to see her soon? Surely, she must know how impatiently I was waiting! She would not be the last of her tribe to reappear!

That night I had but little sleep; excited visions of Yasma permitted me to doze away only by brief dream-broken snatches. But when the gray of dawn began to creep in through the open window, sheer weariness forced an hour's slumber; and I slept beyond my usual time, and awoke to find the room bright with sunlight.

As I opened my eyes, I became conscious of voices without— murmuring voices that filled me with an unreasoning joy. I peered out of the window—no one to be seen! Excitedly I slipped on my coat, and burst out of the door—still no one visible! Then from behind one of the cabins came the roar of half a dozen persons in hearty laughter ... laughter that was the most welcome I had ever heard.

I did not pause to ask myself who the newcomers were; did not stop to wonder whether there were any feminine members of the group. I dashed off crazily, and in an instant found myself confronted by—five or six curiously staring men.

I know that I was indeed a sight; that my eyes bulged; that surprise and disappointment shone in every line of my face. Otherwise, the men would have been quicker to greet me, for instantly we recognized each other. They were youths of the Ibandru tribe, all known to me from last autumn; and they seemed little changed by their long absence, except that, like Julab and Karem, they appeared a trifle thinner.

"Are there any more of you here?" I demanded, after the first words of explanation and welcome. "Are there—are there any—"

Curious smiles flickered across their faces.

"No, it is not quite time yet for the women," one of them replied, as if reading my thoughts. "We men must come first to break the soil and put the village in readiness."

If I had been of no practical use to the Ibandru in the fall, I was to be plunged into continuous service this spring. Daily now I repeated that first afternoon's help I had lent Karem in the fields; and when I did not serve Karem himself, I aided one of his tribesmen, working from sunrise to sunset with occasional intervals of rest.

It was well that I had this occupation, for it tended to keep me sane. After three or four days, my uneasiness would have amounted to agony had my labors not provided an outlet. For I kept looking for one familiar form; and that form did not appear. More than twenty of the men had returned, but not a single woman or child; and I had the dull tormenting sense that I might not see Yasma for weeks yet.

This was the thought that oppressed me one morning when I began tilling a little patch of land near the forest edge. My implements were of the crudest, a mere shovel and spade to break the soil in primitive fashion; and as I went through the laborious motions, my mind was less on the task I performed than on more personal things. I could not keep from thinking of Yasma with a sad yearning, wondering as to her continued absence, and offering up silent prayers that I might see her soon again.

And while I bent pessimistically over my spade, a strange song burst forth from the woods, a bird-song trilling with the rarest delicacy and sweetness. Enchanted, I listened; never before had I heard a song of quite that elfin, ethereal quality. I could not recognize from what feathered minstrel it came; I could only stand transfixed at its fluted melody, staring in vain toward the thick masses of trees for a glimpse of the tiny musician.

It could not have been more than a minute before the winged enchantress fell back into silence; but in that time the world had changed. Its black hostility had vanished; a spirit of beauty surrounded me again, and I had an inexplicable feeling that all would be well.

And as I gazed toward the forest, still hopeful of seeing the sweet-voiced warbler, I was greeted by an unlooked-for vision.

Framed in a sort of natural doorway of the woods, where the pale green foliage was parted in a little arched opening, stood a slender figure with gleaming dark eyes and loose-flowing auburn hair.

"Yasma!" I shouted. And my heart pounded as if it would burst; and my limbs shuddered, and my breath came fast; and the silent tears flowed as I staggered forward with outspread arms.

Without a word she glided forth to meet me, and in an instant we were locked in an embrace.

It must have been minutes before we parted. Not a syllable did we speak; ours was a reunion such as sundered lovers may know beyond the grave.

When at length our arms slipped apart and I gazed at the familiar face, her cheeks were wet but her eyes were glistening. It might have been but an hour since we had met, for she did not seem changed at all.

"Oh, my beloved," she murmured, using the first term of endearment I had ever heard from her lips, "it has been so long since I have seen you! So long, oh, how long!"

"It has been long for me too. Longer than whole years. Oh, Yasma, why did you have to leave?"

A frown flitted across the beautiful face, and the luminous eyes became momentarily sad. "Do not ask that!" she begged. "Oh, do not ask now!" And, seeing her distress, I was sorry that the unpremeditated question had slipped from my lips.

"All that counts, Yasma," said I, gently, "is that you are here now. For that I thank whatever powers have had you in their keeping."

"Thank Yulada!" she suggested, cryptically, with a motion toward the southern mountains.

It was now my turn to frown.

"Oh, tell me, tell me all that has happened during the long winter!" she demanded, almost passionately, as I clutched both her hands and she stared up at me with an inquiring gaze. "You look so changed! So worn and tired out, as if you had been through great sufferings! Did you really suffer so much?"

"My greatest suffering, Yasma, was the loneliness I felt for you. That was harder to bear than the blizzards. But, thank heaven! that is over now. You won't ever go away from me again, will you, Yasma?"

She averted her eyes, then impulsively turned from me, and stood staring toward that steel-gray figure on the peak. It was a minute before she faced me again; and when she did so it was with lips drawn and compressed.

"We must not talk of such things!" she urged, with pleading in her eyes. "We must be happy, happy now while we can be, and not question what is to come!"

"Of course, we must be happy now," I agreed. But her reply had aroused my apprehensions, and even at the moment of reunion I wondered whether she had come only to flutter away again like a feather or a cloud.

"See how quick I came back to you!" she cried, as though to divert my mind. "I left before all the other women, for I knew you would be waiting here, lonely for me."

"And were you too lonely, Yasma?"

"Oh, yes! Very lonely! I never knew such loneliness before!" And the great brown eyes again took on a melancholy glow, which brightened into a happy luster as she looked up at me confidently and reassuringly.

"Then let's neither of us be lonely again!" I entreated. And forgetting my spade and shovel and the half-tilled field, I drew her with me into the seclusion of the woods, and sat down with her by a bed of freshly uncurling ferns beneath the shaded bole of a great oak.

"Remember, Yasma," I said, while I held both her hands and she peered at me out of eyes large with emotion, "you made me a promise about the spring. I asked you a question—the most important question any human being can ask another—and you did not give me a direct answer, but promised you would let me know when the leaves were again sprouting on the trees. That time has come now, and I am anxious for my answer, because I have had long, so very long to wait."

Again I noticed a constraint about her manner. She hesitated before the first words came; then spoke tremblingly and with eyes downcast.

"I know that you have had long to wait, and I do not want to keep you in suspense! I wish I could answer you now, answer outright, so that there would never be another question—but oh, I cannot!—not yet, not yet! Please don't think I want to cause you pain, for there's no one on earth I want less to hurt! Please!"—And she held out her hands imploringly, and her fingers twitched, and deep agitated streams of red coursed to her cheeks.

"I know you don't want to hurt me—" I assured her.

But she halted me with a passionate outburst.

"All I know is that I love you, love you, love you!" she broke out, with the fury of a vehement wild thing; and for a moment we were again clasped in a tight embrace.

"But if you love me, Yasma," I pleaded, when her emotion had nearly spent itself, "why treat me so oddly? Why not be perfectly frank? I love you too, Yasma. Why not say you will be my wife? For I want you with me always, always! Oh, I'd gladly live with you here in Sobul—but if we could we'd go away, far, far away, to my own land, and see things you never saw in your strangest dreams! What do you say, Yasma?"

Yasma said nothing at all. She sat staring straight ahead, her fingers folding and unfolding over some dead twigs, her lips drawn into rigid lines that contrasted strangely with her moist eyes and cheeks.

"You promised that in the spring you would tell me," I reminded her, gently.

I do not know what there was in these words to arouse her to frenzy. Abruptly she sprang to her feet, all trace of composure gone; her eyes blazed with unaccountable fires as she hurled forth her answer.

"Very well then, I will tell you! I cannot say yes to you, and I cannot say no—I cannot, cannot! Go see my father, Abthar, as soon as he returns— he will tell you! Go see him—and Hamul-Kammesh, the soothsayer."

"Why Hamul-Kammesh?"

"Don't ask me—ask them!" she cried, with passion. "I've told you all I can! You'll find out, you'll find out soon enough!"

To my astonishment, her fury was lost amid a tumult of sobbing. No longer the passionate woman but the heart-broken child, she wept as though she had nothing more to live for; and when I came to her consolingly, she flung convulsive arms about me, and clung to me as though afraid I would vanish. And then, while the storm gradually died down and her slender form shook less spasmodically and the tears flowed in dwindling torrents, I whispered tender and soothing things into her ear; but all the time a new and terrible dread was in my heart, for I was certain that Yasma had not told me everything, but that her outburst could be explained only by some close-guarded and dire secret.

CHAPTER XIV
THE WARNING

H ad it been possible to consult Abthar immediately in the effort to fathom Yasma's strange conduct, I would have wasted only so much time as was necessary to take me to the father's cabin. But, unfortunately, I must remain in suspense. So far as I knew, Abthar had not yet returned to the village; and none of the townsfolk seemed sure when he would be back. "He will come before the last blossom buds on the wild rose," was the only explanation they would offer; and knowing that it was not the way of the Ibandru to be definite, I had to be content with this response.

True, I might have followed Yasma's suggestion and sought advice of Hamul-Kammesh, since already that Rip Van Winkle figure was to be seen shuffling about the village. But ever since the time, months before, when he had visited my sick-room and denounced me to the people, I had disliked him profoundly; and I would about as soon have thought of consulting a hungry tiger.

And so my only choice was to wait for Abthar's return. The interval could not have been more than a week; but during all that time I suffered torments. How to approach him, after his return, was a question that occupied me continually. Should I ask him bluntly what secret there was connected with Yasma? Or should I be less direct but more open, and frankly describe my feelings? It was only after much thought that I decided that it would be best to come to him candidly as a suitor in quest of his daughter's hand.

I well remember with what mixed feelings I recognized Abthar's tall figure once more in the village. What if, not unlike some western fathers, he should be outraged at the idea of uniting his daughter to an alien? Or what if he should mention some tribal law that forbade my alliance to Yasma? or should inform me that she was already betrothed? These and other possibilities presented themselves in a tormenting succession ... so that, when at length I did see Abthar, I was hampered by a weight of imaginary ills.

As on a previous occasion, I found the old man working among his vines. Bent over his hoe, he was uprooting the weeds so diligently that at first he did not appear to see me; and I had to hail him loudly before he looked up with a start and turned upon me those searching proud brown eyes of his.

We exchanged greetings as enthusiastically as old friends who have not met for some time; while, abandoning his hoe, Abthar motioned me to a seat beside him on a little mound of earth.

For perhaps a quarter of an hour our conversation consisted mostly of questions on his part and answers on mine; for he was eager to know how I had passed the winter, and had no end of inquiries to make.

For my own part, I refrained from asking that question which bewildered me most of all: how had he and his people passed the winter? It was with extreme difficulty that I halted the torrent of his solicitous queries, and informed him that I had a confession to offer and a request to make.

Abthar looked surprised, and added to my embarrassment by stating how gratified he felt that I saw fit to confide in him.

I had to reply, of course, that there was a particular reason for confiding in him, since my confession concerned his daughter Yasma.

"My daughter Yasma?" he repeated, starting up as though I had dealt him a blow. And he began stroking his long grizzled beard solemnly, and the keen inquiring eyes peered at me as though they would bore their way straight through me and ferret out my last thought.

"What about my daughter Yasma?" he asked, after a pause, and in tones that seemed to bristle with just a trace of hostility.

As tranquilly as I could, I explained how much Yasma had come to mean to me; how utterly I was captivated by her, how desirous of making her my wife. And, concluding with perhaps more tact than accuracy, I remarked that in coming to him to request the hand of his daughter, I was taking the course considered proper in my own country.

In silence Abthar heard me to the last word. He did not interrupt when I paused as if anxious for comment; did not offer so much as a syllable's help when I hesitated or stammered; did not permit any emotion to cross his weather-beaten bronzed features. But he gazed at me with a disquieting fixity and firmness; and the look in his alert stern eyes showed that he had not missed a gesture or a word.

Even after I had finished, he sat regarding me contemplatively without speaking. Meanwhile my fingers twitched; my heart thumped at a telltale speed; I felt like a prisoner arraigned before the bar. But he, the judge, appeared unaware of my agitation, and would not break my suspense until he had fully decided upon his verdict.

Yet his first words were commonplace enough.

"I had never expected anything at all like this," he said, in low sad tones. "Nothing like this has ever been known among our people. We Ibandru have seen little of strangers; none of our young people have ever taken mates outside the tribe. And so your confession comes as a shock."

"It should not come as a shock," was all I could mumble in reply.

"Were I as other fathers," continued the old man, suavely, "I might rise up and order you expelled from our land. Or I might grow angry and shout, and forbid you to see my daughter again. Or I might be crafty, and ask you to engage in feats of prowess with the young men of the town—and so might prove your unworthiness. Or I might send your request to the tribal council, which would decide against you. But I shall do none of these things. Once I too was young, and once I too—" here his voice faltered, and his eyes grew soft with reminiscence—"once I too knew what it was to love. So I shall try not to be too harsh, my friend. But you ask that which I fear is impossible. For your sake, I am sorry that it is impossible. But it is my duty to show you why."

During this speech my heart had sunk until it seemed dead and cold within me. It was as if a world had been shattered before my eyes; as if in the echoes of my own thoughts I heard that fateful word, "Impossible, impossible, impossible!"

"There are so many things to consider, so many things you cannot even know," Abthar proceeded, still stroking his beard meditatively, while my restless fingers toyed with the clods of earth, and my eyes followed absently the wanderings of an ant lost amid those mountainous masses. "But let me explain as well as I can. I shall try to talk to you as a friend, and forget for the time that I am Yasma's father. I shall say nothing of my hopes for her, and how I always thought to see her happy with some sturdy young tribesman, with my grandchildren upon her knee. I shall say nothing of the years that are past, and how I have tried to do my best for her, a motherless child; how sometimes I blundered and sometimes misunderstood, and was more anxious about her and more blest by her than you or she will ever know. Let that all be forgotten. What concerns us now is that you are proposing to make both her and yourself more unhappy than any outcast."

"Unhappy!" I exclaimed, with an unconscious gesture to the blue skies to witness how I was misjudged. "Unhappy! May the lightning strike me down if I don't want to make her happier than a queen!"

"So you say," replied the old man, with just the hint of a cynical smile, "and so you no doubt believe. We all set out in life to make ourselves and others happy—and how many of us succeed? Just now, Yasma's blackest enemy could not do her greater mischief."

"Oh, don't say that!" I protested, clenching my fists with a show of anger. "Have you so far misunderstood me? Do you believe that I—that I—"

"I believe your motives are of the worthiest," interrupted Abthar, quietly. "But let us be calm. It is not your fault that your union with Yasma would be a mistake; circumstances beyond all men's control would make it so."

"What circumstances?"

"Many circumstances. Some of them concern only you; some only Yasma. But suppose we begin with you. I will forget that Yasma and I really know very little about you; about your country, your people, your past. I am confident of your good faith; and for that reason, and because I consider you my friend, I do not want to see you beating your heart out on the rocks. Yet what would happen? Either you would find your way back to your own land and take Yasma with you, or else you would live with her in Sobul. And either course would be disastrous.

"Let us first say that you took her with you to your own country. I have heard only vague rumors as to that amazing land; but I am certain what its effect would be. Have you ever seen a wild duck with a broken wing, or a robin in a cage? Have you ever thought how a doe must feel when it can no longer roam the fields, or an eagle when barred from the sky? Think of these, and then think how Yasma will be when the lengthening days can no longer bring her back to Sobul!"

The old man paused, and with an eloquent gesture pointed to the jagged, snow-streaked circle of the peaks and to the far-off, mysterious figure of Yulada.

"Yes, yes, I have thought of that," I groaned.

"Then here is what we must expect. If you should take Yasma with you to your own country, she would perish—yes, she would perish no matter how kind you were to her, for endless exile is an evil that none of us Ibandru can endure. Yet if you remained with her in Sobul, you would be exiled from your own land and people."

"That is only too true," I sighed, for the thought was not exactly new to me.

But at that instant I chanced to catch a distant glimpse of an auburn-haired figure lithely skirting the further fields; and the full enchantment of Yasma was once more upon me.

"It would be worth the exile!" I vowed, madly. "Well, well worth it! For Yasma's sake, I'd stay here gladly!"

"Yes, gladly," repeated the old man, with a sage nod. "I know you would stay here gladly—for a while. But it would not take many years, my friend, not many years before you would be weary almost to death of this quiet little valley and its people. Why, you would be weary of us now were it not for Yasma. And then some day, when unexpectedly you found the route back to your own world, you would pick up your things and silently go."

"Never! By all I have ever loved, I could not!" I swore. "Not while Yasma remained!"

"Very well, let us suppose you would stay here," conceded Abthar, hastily, as though skimming over a distasteful topic. "Then if your life were not ruined, Yasma's would be. There are reasons you may not be aware of."

"There seems to be much here that I am not aware of."

"No doubt," Abthar admitted, in matter-of-fact tones. And then, with a gesture toward the southern peak, "Yulada has secrets not for every man's understanding."

For an instant he paused, in contemplation of the statue-like figure; then quickly continued, "Now here, my friend, is the thing to remember. Take the migration from which we are just returning. Do not imagine that we make such a pilgrimage only once in a lifetime. Every autumn, when the birds fly south, we follow in their wake; and every spring we return with the northward-winging flocks."

"Every autumn—and every spring!" I gasped, in dismay, for Abthar had confirmed my most dismal surmises.

"Yes, every autumn and every spring. How would you feel, my friend, with a wife that left you five months or six every year? How do you think your wife would feel when she had to leave?"

"But would she have to leave? Why would she? After we were married, would she not be willing to stay here?"

"She might be willing—but would she be able?" asked Abthar, pointedly. "This is no matter of choice; it is a law of her nature. It is a law of the nature of all Ibandru to go every autumn the way of the south-ward-speeding birds. Could you ask the sap to stop flowing from the roots of the awakening tree in April? Could you ask the fountains not to pour down from the peaks when spring thaws the snow? Then ask one of us Ibandru to linger in Sobul when the frosty days have come and the last November leaf flutters earthward."

Abthar's words bewildered me utterly, as all reference to the flight of the Ibandru had bewildered me before. But I did not hesitate to admit my perplexity. "Your explanation runs contrary to all human experience," I argued. "During my studies and travels, I have heard of many races of men who differed much in habits and looks; but all were moved by the same impulses, the same natural laws. You Ibandru alone seem different. You disappear and reappear like phantoms, and claim to do so because of an instinct never found in the natural world."

My companion sat staring at me quizzically. There was just a little of surprise in his manner, just a little of good-natured indulgence, and something of the smiling tolerance which one reserves for the well-meaning and simple-minded.

"In spite of your seeming knowledge, my friend," he remarked at length, "I see that you are really quite childish in your views. You are mistaken in believing that we Ibandru do not follow natural laws. We are guided not by an instinct unknown in the great world around us, but by one that rules the lives of countless living things: the birds in the air and the fishes in the streams, and even, if I am to believe the tales I have heard, is found among certain furry animals in the wide waters and at times among swarms of butterflies."

"But if you feel the same urge as these creatures, then why should only you out of all men feel it?"

"No doubt it exists elsewhere, although weakened by unnatural ways of life. Did it ever occur to you that it may have been common to all men thousands of years ago? Did you never stop to think that you civilized folk may have lost it, just as you have lost your keenness of scent and sense of direction? while we Ibandru have preserved it by our isolation and the simplicity of our lives? As your own fathers may have been five hundred generations ago, so we Ibandru are today."

"But if your migration be a natural thing," I asked, remembering the sundry mysteries of Sobul, "why make a secret of it? Why not tell me where you go in winter? Indeed, why not take me with you?"

A strange light came into Abthar's eyes. There was something a little secretive and yet something a little exalted in his manner as he lifted both hands ardently toward Yulada, and declared, "There are truths of which I dare not speak, truths that the tradition of my tribe will not let me reveal. But do not misunderstand me, my friend; we must keep our secrets for the sake of our own safety as well as because of Yulada. If all that we do were known to the world, would we not be surrounded by curious and unkindly throngs? Hence our ancient sages ordained that when we Ibandru go away at the time of falling leaves we must go alone, unless there be with us some understanding stranger—one who has felt the same inspiration as we. But such a stranger has never appeared. And until he does appear, Yulada will weave dread spells over him who betrays her secrets!"

The old man paused, and I had no response to make.

"But all this is not what you came to see me about," he continued. "Let us return to Yasma. Now that I have told you of our yearly migration, you can judge of the folly you were contemplating. But let me mention another fact, which even by itself would make your marriage foolhardy."

"What fact can that be?" I demanded, feeling as if a succession of hammer strokes had struck me on the head.

"Again I must go out of my way to explain. For many generations, as far back as our traditions go, there has been one of our number known as a soothsayer, a priest of Yulada. His mission is to read the omens of earth and sky, to scan the clouds and stars, and to tell us Yulada's will. Sometimes his task has been difficult, for often Yulada has hidden behind a mist; but at other times his duty has been clear as light, and we have profited greatly from his wisdom. Yulada has never been known to betray her worshipper; all those who have heeded her have been blest, and all the scorners have lived to rue their scorn. And so, for hundreds of years, as far back as we can remember, whenever Hamul-Kammesh has foretold—"

"But how old under heaven is Hamul-Kammesh?"

"As old as the Ibandru," stated Abthar, simply. "As old as Yulada herself. The physical form changes, but Hamul-Kammesh is always the same. The father dies, and the son takes his place; but still we call him Hamul-Kammesh, for still he is the mouthpiece of Yulada."

"Maybe so," I conceded. "But what has all this to do with Yasma?"

"More than I wish it had! More than I wish!" declared Yasma's father, gloomily. "At the time of her birth a prophecy was made—"

"Prophecy?"

"Yes, a bitter prophecy! I well recall the day; the wild geese were flying south, and Yulada's head and shoulders were hooded in gray cloud. In that cloud a slit appeared and vanished; but we could see that it took the form of a man—a man striding toward us from across the mountains. At the same time, a flock of seventeen birds went winging above the peak; so that Hamul-Kammesh, reflecting upon these omens, was led to foretell a sad fate for the babe born on that day. After seventeen summers, he said, a stranger would come to us from beyond the mountains; and he would mean us no harm, and would have to be respected, yet would work grievous ill; for his fate was darkly connected with that of Yasma, my child. How it was connected, Hamul-Kammesh did not say; but the sun that day at twilight was strangely red through the western mist; and in the deep crimson dusk the soothsayer saw disaster. Nevertheless, he warned us that we could not struggle against that disaster; it was foreordained, and was the will of Yulada!"

A long, painful silence followed, which I did not choose to break. For Abthar had spoken in the tones of one who dwells on tragedy that has been no less than on tragedy to be; and his eyes, so keen and alert before, now bore the weary look of one who tells for the hundredth time an old hopeless tale.

"For years I rarely thought of that prediction," he finally resumed. "We are all apt to forget the fate that hovers above us. Even when you were first carried into our midst, I did not connect your arrival with Hamul-Kammesh's prophecy. In fact, no one connected the two events until the soothsayer himself spoke of you as the stranger whose coming he had divined long ago. Then to the old forecasts he added new ... but these I need not mention. The meaning of it all, is this: should you wed Yasma, you will court your own doom. That is all I need to say. If, knowing what you know, you must persist in your madness, I will lift my voice no further; but the blame for your sufferings will not be mine."

"Oh, but how can you expect me to believe such predictions?" I protested, more impressed than I would have admitted even to myself. "How can you—"

I could proceed no further. "That is all, my friend," said Abthar, with decision. "Perhaps some other time we shall have further talk."

Solemnly he arose, and slowly went ambling away among the green rows of vines, his great graying head bent sadly and thoughtfully over his long lanky form.

CHAPTER XV
CRUCIAL MOMENTS

H ad I been the man that I was before my arrival in Sobul, I should not have thought twice about Abthar's warnings. I should have laughed at them as the wild imaginings of a primitive folk, and should have gone my way regardless of his beliefs. But I was no longer the same man as upon my arrival. My years of civilization were overcast and obscured; so much of the seemingly miraculous had occurred that I was in a mood to expect miracles. And so, when Abthar informed me of the prophecies and the peril of marrying Yasma, it was not my full heart and soul that rose up in revolt; my intellect did indeed protest, but not with the courage of utter conviction; for an insinuating voice kept whispering sly doubts and suspicions. What if some dismal fortune should actually await me if I scorned Abthar's advice? What if I should endanger my beloved? What if the tribe's disapproval, or the tribe's superstition, or some sort of social ostracism, should pave the way for tragedy? Or what if Yasma's own fears, or her passionate religious scruples, or her peculiar training and habits of thought, should precipitate disaster?

Such were my thoughts as I sadly wandered back to my cabin after the interview with Abthar. I was at the bleakest point of my reveries when I heard a familiar voice hailing me cheerfully, and looked up to find a brawny hand slapping me companionably on the shoulder and two glittering black eyes staring inquiringly into mine.

"Tell me, what's wrong with the world today?" exclaimed Karem, gaily, as he fell in at my side. "You looked so sad I thought you might be needing a friend."

"I certainly am needing a friend," I acknowledged. And, eager for sympathy, I told of my interview with his father, laying particular stress on what had been said of Hamul-Kammesh and his prophecies.

Karem followed me attentively, but the sparkle never left his eyes.

"Yes, I've heard all about Hamul-Kammesh," he declared, quietly, when I had finished. "Especially about his prophecies, which have given him great fame. But I would not take them too seriously, if I were you."

"Your father seems to take them very seriously."

"Yes, of course, father would," remarked Karem, pointedly. "All the more so, since he wants to keep you from my sister."

"So you don't think there's anything in them?"

"Oh, I would not say that. There is just as much in them as you want to see—and just as little. The old folks would chop off their hands if Hamul-Kammesh told them to, but we younger Ibandru—well, we younger Ibandru sometimes have our doubts."

"I see," said I, glad to know that youth could be skeptical even in Sobul. "But your father tells me that Hamul-Kammesh's prophecies always come true."

Karem looked across at me with an ingenuous smile.

"So they will all tell you. But that too depends upon what you want to believe. Naturally, Hamul-Kammesh had to make a prediction when Yasma was born; he's expected to make a prediction at the time of every birth. So as to be sure of himself, he foretold something that was not to happen for seventeen years, when everyone would have forgotten just what he said. Then, again, he said a stranger was coming to Sobul, and there too he was safe, because if no man had appeared there would certainly have been some male babe born during the year; and then Hamul-Kammesh would have said that that babe was the man he meant in his prophecy, but we should have to wait twenty years more until the man was grown up and the prediction could come true. Of course, when you unexpectedly arrived, he recognized his opportunity, and claimed to have foreseen your coming seventeen years before."

"Nevertheless," I contended, doubtfully, "it *is* a strange coincidence, is it not?"

"If it were not for coincidences, Prescott, soothsayers would have to pass their days tilling the soil like the rest of us!"

Thereupon Karem made an eloquent gesture toward the unplanted fields, where a score of men were bent low with spades and shovels. And, telling me that he had been idle too long already, he left me to my ruminations.

But the effect of our conversation had been to lift me out of my dejection. I could no longer trouble myself about the old medicine-man and his predictions; could no longer believe that some dire fate hovered over us; could no longer feel my union with Yasma to be impossible. Whatever the obstacles, they were of a calculable and natural character; and whatever the dangers, they were not too great to confront and overcome. Reconsidering my problems in the light of Karem's wisdom, I determined to face the prospect of marriage with Yasma just as I might have faced a similar prospect with a girl of my own race; I resolved to go to her at once, to put the entire question before her, to reason with her, to plead with her, to overwhelm her objections, to wrest a promise from her, and so to fight my way to the speedy and triumphant consummation of our love.

The crucial moment was not long in coming. The next morning I went to see Yasma at her father's cabin; and finding her preparing to set out all alone for the woods, I invited myself to join her. Soberly we started out together while I chatted about trifles, as if unaware of the all-important turning point just ahead.—But could it be that the next few hours would mark the climax of both our lives?

We had strolled perhaps two or three miles when we paused in a little wildflower glade beside a sunlit brook. With a cry of delight at the deep blue of the skies and the delicate immature green of the encircling foliage, Yasma threw herself down in the grass; and, not awaiting her invitation, I seated myself at her side.

For several minutes neither of us spoke. The rivulet trickled along its way; bird called merrily to bird from unseen fastnesses in the treetops; the first butterfly of the season went flapping past on wings of white and yellow. And bird and butterfly and stream might have been the sole subjects of our thoughts.

Yet all the while my mind was busy—and busy not with dreams of blue skies or growing leaves or ripening blossoms.

"Do you know, Yasma," I finally began, while she sat wistfully gazing toward the woods, "I was speaking to your father yesterday."

"Yes?" she murmured, in barely audible tones. To judge by the faint-heartedness of her response, she might not have been interested; yet I noticed that she gave a slight start and bent her head away from me, while her fingers absently fondled the grass.

"Yes; I was speaking to your father," I repeated, my eyes intently upon her. "Remember, you advised me to. I am glad that I did, for now everything seems clearer."

"Clearer?" she asked, doubtfully, as she turned her gaze full upon me. "What is clearer?"

For an instant I flinched before that steady, questioning glance.

"It is clearer, how we two should act. Let us not blind ourselves with doubts, Yasma, nor throw our lives away over childish fancies. I have considered everything; I have thought and thought, and cannot see any objections great enough to stand in the way of our love. Let us pay no heed to what anyone may say; we shall be married, you and I; yes, we shall—"

Yasma had sprung to her feet; with a furious exclamation, she interrupted me. "No, no, no! It cannot be!"

In quivering agitation, she started pacing about the glade; and I had to go to her, and take her hands, and lead her back to her deserted grassy seat.

"Now we must talk things over calmly, Yasma," I urged. "Your father and I have talked them over calmly. And we have agreed quite well."

"But he didn't agree to let you marry me?" she demanded, almost fiercely. "He didn't agree to that?"

"He gave me his advice, and said everything was in our own hands."

"What advice did he give?" she flashed at me, not to be put off by equivocations. And her dark eyes shone with such distress that I would gladly have ended all arguments in a swift embrace.

But I understood the need to state the facts unemotionally. As simply as I could, I reported the general drift of my conversation with Abthar.

"You see!" she flung forth, when I had finished. "You see! It cannot be!" And again she arose; and wringing her hands like one who has suffered vile misfortune, she retreated to the further end of the glade.

And again I had to go to her and lead her gently back to her seat by the rivulet's brink.

"Let us be calm, Yasma," I pleaded once more. "There is no reason why we cannot have everything we wish. We shall yet be happy together, you and I."

"Happy? How can we be?" she lamented as her moist eyes stared at me with unfathomable sadness. "You are not as I—you cannot go with me each year when the birds fly south."

For a moment I did not reply. I had the curious impression of being like the hero of some old fairy tale, a man wedded to a swallow or a wild duck in human form.

"If I could not go with you," I entreated, though I felt the hopelessness of my own words, "why could you not stay here? Surely, if we were married, you might remain."

"Oh, I would if I could," she cried, clasping her hands together fervently, and peering in despair toward the remote figure of Yulada. "I would if I could!" And she bent her head low, and her clenched fists hid her eyes, and her whole slender form shuddered.

"Yasma!" I murmured, with an echo of her own emotion, as I took her into my arms.

But she broke away from me savagely. "No, no, you must not!" she protested, her eyes gleaming and angry, her flushed cheeks newly wet.

"But why not? Why—"

"Because you and I are not the same! You do not know, you do not know what it is to hear the call of Yulada, to feel the fire burning, thundering in your veins, forcing you away when the leaves turn red, forcing you away, over the mountains, far, far away!"

"I do not know, Yasma, but could I not learn?"

"You could not learn! Once I hoped so, but I do not now! Can the bird raised in a cage learn to travel in the skies? You could not learn! It is too late! Each year I must go away, but always you must stay here!"

"Even so, Yasma, let us not be sad. I would have you six months each year, and that would be far, far better than not to have you at all."

"So you say," she murmured, looking up at me with wide, yearning eyes. "So you say now. But when the time came for me to leave, would you be contented? Rather, would you not be the most miserable man in the world?"

"But why should I be miserable? Would I not know you were coming back? Is it so terrible there where you go in the winter?"

"No, it is not terrible. It is beautiful."

"Then for your sake, I would reconcile myself. If you were happy, why should I not be?"

"Because you are not made that way! No, you could not be happy, my friend," she continued, staring at me with a melancholy smile. "And perfectly dreadful things might happen."

Long, long afterwards, when it was too late for anything but memories, I was to recall those words. But at the moment I brushed them aside, for there in those peaceful woods, with the birds singing in the treetops and the clear warm skies above, I did not believe that anything dreadful could happen to Yasma or myself.

"If I am willing to endure your absence," I appealed, "then what should be your objections? If those are your only reasons, let us prepare for the wedding!"

"You know those are not my only reasons," she denied, almost reproachfully. "You know there are a hundred other reasons! Now that you have heard of the prophecies—"

"The prophecies mean nothing!" I asserted, emboldened by my talk with Karem. "They are mere guesses! They will not come true!"

"What!" she flung back, horrified at this blasphemy. "You say Hamul-Kammesh's prophecies will not come true?"

"No, Yasma, they are only meant to frighten us. Let us not be misled by fairy tales."

"Fairy tales, you call them?"—Her attitude had become almost defiant.—"You do not know much of Hamul-Kammesh, or you would not speak so foolishly."

"All that I know," I acknowledged, letting just a trace of irony creep into my words, "is that he is supposed to be the earthly agent of Yulada."

"He is more than that. He is her seer, her prophet, her law-giver, her tool of vengeance! Her will is his will! When he speaks, it is she that addresses us! Why, you do not know of the wonders, the wonders he has done, the wise things he has said!"

"No, I do not know."

"You have not heard how once he predicted disaster, and twenty people were smitten with the plague! And, again, how he foretold a rich season, and our harvests were the most bountiful we had ever known! And how he prayed in time of drought, and the rain came; and how he spoke to the waters when we feared a spring flood, and the waters shrank back! No, you know nothing of Hamul-Kammesh! You cannot appreciate his miracles! You are not to be blamed for scorning him, since you have had no chance to learn!"

"I wish no chance to learn! His prophecies are against all reason!"

"Against all reason or not," she maintained, in the tone of one who proclaims incontrovertible truth, "I know he does not predict falsely. I am sure, oh, I am sure nothing good could come if we two—"

"All things good would come," I pleaded, "if you could forget him and remember only our love." And, drawing close and letting my arms glide about her, I repeated, "Remember only our love. For its sake, would you not take any risk?"

"But not this, not this!" she cried, like one fighting a battle with herself, as she withdrew hastily from my embrace. "Oh, not this! I cannot risk ruining your life and mine! I cannot risk father's anger—the anger of the village, the hatred of Hamul-Kammesh! No, I cannot make you suffer as you would have to do! I cannot bring down the wrath of Yulada! I cannot! There is no more to say! This is final!"

"Final?" I demanded, reeling as if beneath a blow, as I peered into those eyes moist with suffering yet fiery with a new resolution.

"Yes, final!" she affirmed, in the manner of one who forces down a bitter draught. "Final! There can be no other way!"

"Very well, then!" I burst forth, springing to my feet with all the fury of my outraged feelings and balked desires. "Final, let us say that this is final! Final that you will be ruled by a whim! Final that you won't have the courage to fight for your own happiness, or care how my happiness is dragged down! Very well then, let that be! I accept your decision—let this be the final word between us! But I cannot live without you! Tomorrow I leave your valley—yes, leave it not knowing where I go; it does not matter where! I may be lost in the mountains and starve, or stumble over a precipice, or be torn to death by wild beasts—it does not matter! Nothing matters, nothing but you! Good-bye, Yasma!"

Turning my back upon her, I started toward the village.

For a moment all was silent behind me. Then the stillness of the woods was broken by a sob. Startled, I wheeled about; then strode back, and in an instant had my arms about the yielding, convulsive form of Yasma.

"Oh, do not go away!" she wailed. "Do not go away from me, ever, ever! You are everything to me, everything! Oh, what does anything else matter? Let them warn me, forbid me, predict horrible things—I do not care! Nothing could be more horrible than to have you go away! Oh, if I knew I would be smitten dead for it tomorrow, I would still want you here today!"

Again she broke into a passion of tears, which I soothed away as best I could, though I too was near to weeping. But after her emotion had subsided and she could talk calmly again, we sat side by side in the glade for hours, discussing in whispers that which brought happy smiles to our faces and sent a wistful light into her eyes, and also a light of hope.

CHAPTER XVI
HAMUL-KAMMESH ORDAINS

E ven after Yasma and I had agreed, it was no easy matter to carry out our plans. We foresaw that most of the villagers would be unalterably prejudiced; that they would regard our union as impious; that Hamul-Kammesh would fan their opposition and refuse to perform the ceremony; that, even were we wedded, we should be in danger of living as outcasts, since in Sobul it was virtually necessary to secure the community's consent to a marriage.

After racking my brains for hours, I decided to consult Karem; and, accordingly, I went to him where he was working in the fields, and declared that I desired his advice on an important matter.

Karem seemed not at all surprised, but continued to plunge his spade methodically into the earth. "I shall help you—if I can," was all he said.

As calmly as I could, I explained about Yasma, emphasizing the need of having our relationship accepted in the village.

All the while that I was talking, Karem remained busy at his spade; yet his bronzed brow was ruffled with thought.

"You have not an easy fight to win," he reminded me, when I had finished. And he paused in his labors, and stood with one hand clutching the wooden spade-handle, and one hand meditatively propping up his chin. "Still, there must be ways. If you can only gain the favor of Hamul-Kammesh, the others will follow fast enough."

"Yes, but how gain the favor of Hamul-Kammesh? Certainly, he won't consent out of love for me. And I don't happen to have—well, anything valuable—"

"Oh, you shouldn't have to bribe him," interrupted Karem, reflectively. "You will only have to make him friendly out of self-defense. If he has to smile upon your marriage for the sake of his prestige, be sure he will smile his brightest."

"But how could my marriage affect his prestige?"

"We must, of course, strike at his most vital spots. And the most vital spots are his miracles, prophecies, and dreams.... Now do you see?"

"I'm afraid I don't."

"Hamul-Kammesh claims to be a great interpreter of dreams," continued my friend, with mounting enthusiasm, while the spade-handle dropped unheeded to the ground. "He is honored as much for his dream-readings as for his prophecies. Not only our own Hamul-Kammesh but all his ancestors for a hundred generations have been dream-readers. They have construed so many dreams that they have come to have a code; this applies to all the every-day dreams, and is known to the whole tribe. Thus, if you dream you are attacked by wild beasts, this means that evil spirits are abroad and disease will break out in the village. Or, if you dream of falling from a treetop, this means that someone will be stricken dead unless we propitiate Yulada. Or, again, if your dream is of comets or shooting stars, this is proof that the gods are conferring and a great leader is to be born among us."

"All very interesting!" I commented, beginning to see the light. "But just how does it concern us now?"

"I thought you would have guessed," declared Karem, with a tinge of disappointment. "Then consider this: if you dream that you see two white clouds, and the clouds travel side by side through blue skies, the explanation is that there is soon to be a marriage in the village. Now what if I were to dream about two such clouds?"

"Oh, so that's it!" I shot out, laughing heartily at Karem's naïve way of putting the idea. "So you can dream to order?"

"Why not? It has been done before."

"And you have often dreamed—"

"No, not I. If I had dreamed too often, the people might lose faith in me. As it is, I am not free to doubt the dreams of my friends. Why should they doubt mine?"

"Then how will you arrange things?"

Karem smiled a broad, knowing smile. "Oh, that will be as easy as burning dry straw. I will whisper to some of my friends about the two white clouds. But only in confidence. I will ask them not to let anyone know. Within a day or two, twenty people will come to Hamul-Kammesh secretly with the story of the dream. They will all want to know who's going to get married. That will make the soothsayer wrinkle up his brows, because none of our young people are to be married just now—most of our matings, you know, take place at the harvest time, when the year's labors are about over. Naturally, Hamul will look wise on hearing of the dream, and will make some prophecies, but at the same time he will be worried, because his reputation will be threatened. Then, just when he is hardest put to find a way out, I will see him and mention that you hope to marry my sister. This will give him his chance, and he will proclaim that your marriage to Yasma has been ordered by Yulada, and preparations must be made immediately."

"That sounds logical enough," I admitted. "But can the people all be duped so easily?"

"No, not all. But many can. And those who are not deceived will be too wise to seem to doubt."

My only reply was an ironic nod.

Four or five days after my talk with Karem, I received a visitor who had never favored me before. I had just returned from the fields after a strenuous day's labor, when I observed a tall, long-bearded man framed in the open doorway of my cabin. From his stiff demeanor, as well as from the high black headgear that added a foot to his stature, I recognized him as the soothsayer. Hence I lost no time about inviting him in.

"To what do I owe this honor?" I asked, trying to assume a tone of proper deference.

"My son, I would have a word with you," he began, in a ringing, pompous manner; while, remembering the native etiquette, I motioned him to a seat opposite me on the straw-covered floor.

"Yes, I have an announcement of importance," he continued, as he squatted cross-legged near the door. In the gathering twilight I could not quite make out the expression on his face; but I thought that a troubled look softened his habitual self-satisfaction.

"I shall be flattered!" I stated, bowing almost to the floor according to the local custom.

A silence intervened. Then the soothsayer coughed, cleared his throat, and slowly and with great dignity announced, "It is an extraordinary mission, my son, that brings me here. I come not of my own will, but as the messenger of higher powers. For the gaze of Yulada has alighted upon you, and she has taken pleasure in you and found you worthy, and has decided to bestow a favor upon you."

"A favor?" I echoed, trying to appear surprised. "What favor would Yulada bestow upon one so humble?"

"It is not for us to question the will of those on high," dogmatized the soothsayer, with a pious gesture toward the ceiling. "Nor must we rejoice too much in the moment's happiness, for dark secrets lurk behind the veil, dark secrets lurk behind the veil, and all may not be well hereafter!"

Hamul-Kammesh paused, as though he wished to allow this bit of wisdom time to seep in.

"What dark secrets do you refer to, worthy sire?" I asked, using the native form of address.

"It does not matter, my son. Let us pass them by!" he urged, with a grimace suggesting that he wished to be done with a distasteful topic. "Let us not be concerned with tomorrow's bitter draught till tomorrow is here. At present, we may consider only your good fortune. For Yulada has singled you out for rare good fortune."

"Indeed?"

"Indeed, my son! She has bidden you to smile upon a certain young maiden of our village, and has bidden that maiden to smile back upon you. Her name I need not mention, but it is the desire of Yulada that you woo this daughter of our tribe."

Upon hearing this announcement, I tried not to appear too jubilant.

"If it be the desire of Yulada," I acquiesced, in my most solemn tones, "then who am I to object? My own will is as nothing; I can only humbly offer my thanks, and accept whatever is granted."

"Your spirit does you great credit, young man," approved Hamul-Kammesh, as with a sigh of relief he arose to leave. "I am glad to find that you have a proper humility."

It was fortunate that the darkness was now so deep that the soothsayer could not see my face.

"There is only one thing more," Hamul-Kammesh announced, as he stood again in the doorway. "Yulada decrees that your nuptials take place very soon. Yes, she decrees them at the time of the next full-moon. You will be ready then, my son?"

"If Yulada decrees, I will be ready," said I, bowing my assent. And as the soothsayer went shuffling away through the lamplit village, I let my eyes travel to a crescent moon low-hanging above the western peaks.

But as I stood there gazing across the valley and meditating upon my good fortune, I was not so exultant as I might have been; it was as if a shadow had passed across my life instead of a happy promise. Now that all appeared to be arranged and my marriage to Yasma was inevitable, the haze of my emotions was momentarily rent; I saw with a dispassionate vision, and asked myself whether it was not insane to link myself to this child of a primitive mountain race. Was it not worse than insane, since she belonged to a tribe that possessed qualities scarcely human, a tribe that seemed akin to the wild goose and the dove? So I questioned, as I had questioned more than once in the past; but now, since the fateful event appeared imminent, my doubts were deeper than ever before, and my fears more acute.

Yet, as always, my hesitancies were whisked aside like dust when my mind framed a picture of Yasma, Yasma as she had radiantly flitted along the dim wooded lanes, Yasma as she had clung to me in a storm of sad emotion. And love, the blinding, all-powerful master, came as always to silence the protests of reason; I was flooded once more with tenderness and yearning, was held once more as in a magic mood; and the little remembered things Yasma had said, and the things Yasma had done, the dimpling smiles that played across her face and even the petulant frowns, her quaint little manner of nodding when happy, the puckish creasing of merriment about the corners of her lips, and the pitiful sadness of her half-closed tearful eyes, had all a part in weaving the halo that enveloped her.

And so it was useless to struggle, useless to seek to unravel that web which time and chance and my own passions had wound about me. Even had I known that Yasma and I were to be wedded and the next moment hurled together over a precipice, I would hardly have had the strength to check our fatal course. No! for the sake of my own peace of mind, as well as because dark and powerful forces were stirring within me, I would have had to yield to the enchantment and fuse the two fierce currents of our lives. And so profound was my longing for Yasma that, despite the moment's misgivings, it seemed that an incalculable epoch must pass before the crescent could expand into the full moon.

CHAPTER XVII
AT THE TIME OF THE FULL MOON

A wedding among the Ibandru is celebrated by twenty-four hours of feasting and rejoicing. All members of the tribe are invited, and all are expected to participate; no one is permitted to labor in the fields or at home; from dawn until dawn the village is delivered into the hands of the merrymakers. Bonfires are lighted at night, and weird and picturesque dances executed; songs are sung by day, and races run, and games of strength and skill find favor; prayers are uttered, orations made, stories told, and poems intoned. And as the supreme mark of the occasion, a privilege that combines pleasure with consecration, the elders of the tribe pass the jugs of "sacru," a local intoxicant made from the roots of a starchy herb; and all are urged to drink out of respect for the wedded pair.

Judged by the quantity of "sacru" consumed when Yasma and I were married, the respect in which we were held was enormous. Had the beverage not been withheld during the first two or three hours of the festivities, many of the reverential ones would not have been in a condition to appreciate anything that went on.

For my own part, I had not the same capacity for pleasure as some of the others; indeed, rarely have I been so uncomfortable as on that day which should have been the happiest of my life. Not that I did not appreciate the importance of the occasion; or that I felt any desire to undo the bond now being irrevocably tied. But the crowds of idlers, staring and staring at Yasma and me as though to swallow us with their eyes, made me feel miserably out of place; and the ceremonies were so curious that I felt like an intruder.

When I awoke after a troubled sleep in the dusk of that unforgettable May morning, I was vaguely aware of the undercurrent of excitement in the village. Even at this hour, the people were abroad; I could hear them moving quickly about, could hear their chattering voices. Without delay, therefore, I arose and dressed in a bright blue and red native costume, Abthar's wedding gift, which he had urged upon me in place of my now ragged civilized garb; then somewhat timidly I stepped out of my cabin.

The first persons I met were Karem and his brother Barkodu, who were standing not twenty paces from my door, as though awaiting me. I observed that long ribbons and tassels of red and yellow hung from their heads and shoulders; while streamers of every conceivable hue—crimson and purple, orange, lavender and green—had been strung during the night from cabin to cabin, giving the village a fantastic and festal appearance.

My two friends greeted me enthusiastically; muttered congratulations; and led me to the cabin where Yasma was expecting my arrival. The bride-to-be was clad in a slender, specially woven robe of sky-blue; and ornaments of a stone like amethyst adorned her hair and shoulders. My heart leapt as she beamed her greeting to me—how dazzling, I thought, how dazzling beyond the most gaudy princess that ever graced a salon! She was paler today than ordinarily; her eyes shone with an unusual timidity; yet there was something ravishingly sweet about her expression, a childlike candor and smiling loveliness that reminded me of a flower just bursting into bloom.

But only for one instant I reveled in the sight of her. Then, though she lingered at my side, she might have been a thousand miles away. Together we were escorted to the open space in the center of the village, where we were hailed by scores of men and women, all bedecked with colored tassels and banners. Amid that staring multitude, each member of which came forth in turn to express the same felicitations in the same words, we had little chance to communicate with one another by so much as a meeting of fingers or a sidelong glance. As best we could, we endured the ordeal;

but I could see that Yasma was being tired out by the innumerable bows she had to make and the innumerable expressions of thanks.

The sun had barely overtopped the eastern peaks when Hamul-Kammesh arrived and the ceremonies began. The soothsayer was especially apparelled for the occasion, and wore white robes that matched his beard, and a two-foot conical white hat that brought me frivolous remembrances. Yet he conducted himself with the august air of the wise men of old, and spoke in the sonorous and measured tones of a patriarch. He was especially impressive when he stationed himself on a little newly reared mound in the middle of the clearing, and, taking a small horn-like instrument from his cloak, blew a blast that brought the noisy, chattering assemblage instantly to order.

"Let us begin by offering thanks to Yulada!" he thundered, as soon as the spectators were giving him their undivided attention.

Instantly the three or four hundred men, women and children threw themselves down upon the ground; stretched themselves full-length with faces turned southward; and mumbled and muttered incoherently.

Of course, I had to prostrate myself along with the crowd, and to join in murmuring the unintelligible jargon. But how thankful I was when the ceremony was over! After this trial, it seemed a relief to listen to Hamul-Kammesh.

"My friends," he proclaimed, in the manner of one who relishes his own eloquence, "we are here today by the decree of Yulada, Yulada whose ways are inscrutable and whose will no man can oppose. Why she has brought us together I may not reveal, nor whether tomorrow she will scourge us with earthquake and lightning. All that she permits me to say is that this moment shall be one of rejoicing, for today we celebrate the union of one of our daughters with a stranger from the lands beyond the mountains. Never before have any of our maidens been wedded except to sons of our own tribe, but let us not question Yulada, who is wiser than all men; let us only give thanks, remembering that whatever she does is for our best."

It will be needless to repeat the remainder of the sermon. It would, in fact, be impossible to do so, for all that I can recall is that the speaker continuously praised Yulada, emphasizing and re-emphasizing his remarks until he had spoken for an hour and said the same thing in twenty ways. Yet the audience listened with mouths agape and staring eyes; and when he had finished, there was an uproar of approving yells and cheers.

Following this frightful pandemonium, Hamul-Kammesh prepared to tie the knot that would make Yasma my wife. In ringing tones he uttered first my name, then hers; and in single file we had to thread our way amid the squatting figures and take our places at the soothsayer's side on the central mound. This was embarrassing enough; but a more embarrassing experience awaited us upon our arrival at what I shall call the stage. No sooner were we within touching distance than the soothsayer, with a wide sweep of his arms, enfolded Yasma in a close embrace. Of course, I realized that this was held essential to the ceremony; but it did seem to me that Hamul-Kammesh was unnecessarily long about releasing Yasma. I was about to cough tactfully when he at length freed her, and, to my disgust, flung his arms in my direction, and for an instant I felt his bristly white beard against my face.

But this time the embrace was not protracted. Indeed, I had no more than realized what was happening, when it was over. And Hamul-Kammesh, with a wry grimace, was again addressing the audience:

"The bride and bridegroom have now been enfolded in the arms of Yulada. They are at last fit to leave their solitary paths; and I am therefore ready to declare their two souls immortally one. But first I must speak of their obligations. They must always hold the name of Yulada in awe, and their children and their children's children must have the fear of Yulada in their hearts. They must not fail in that worship which Yulada commands; they must do deference each year by taking the way of the southward-flying birds if but they hear the call; and, above all, they must not reveal any of Yulada's secrets, and must never approach within five stones' throws of the feet of the goddess. But during all the season of green leaves they must remain in Sobul, tilling the earth as Yulada wishes and roaming her mountains but never defiling her trees or wild things. If so, long life will be theirs, unless—unless—" Here Hamul-Kammesh hesitated, and something menacing came into his tone.—"Unless Yulada should not choose to revoke her old prophecy, but, for reasons which only she can fathom, should send some portent of her wrath."

Crowning this address, Hamul-Kammesh stretched his arms imploringly toward Yulada, and, with eyes upturned, mumbled a prayer. And, after completing his incoherent mutterings, he took my right hand in his left, and Yasma's left hand in his right, and joined our two hands in a not unwilling clasp.

For a moment I fancied that this completed the ceremony, and that, according to the law of Sobul, Yasma and I were now man and wife. But I quickly perceived my error. While my betrothed and I stood with hands interlocked, the soothsayer reached into the folds of his garments and withdrew two little ruby-red stones, which he exhibited high in air.

"Here are the life-stones," he explained, "the gems that show the fusion of the heart's blood. These, in the eyes of Yulada, are the symbols of your union; and these Yulada shall now bestow upon you."

There followed an impressive silence, while Hamul-Kammesh carefully examined the red trinkets. Then, turning to me and holding out the larger of the two tokens, he asked, "Do you, the bridegroom, desire this life-stone? Will you cherish it and preserve it, the sign and consecration of your marriage, the gift of Yulada on your wedding day?"

"I shall be glad to do so."

"Then for you Yulada has tied the cord that cannot be broken!" And, by means of a little projecting hook, the old man fastened the red stone just above my heart.

Then, while the audience stood looking on breathlessly, he turned to Yasma, held forth the second little jewel, and repeated the questions he had asked me.

But what a startling change had come over Yasma! Her face had grown tense and white; her eyes were distended; suddenly she seemed smitten dumb. After Hamul-Kammesh had put the final question, she remained simply staring at him—staring without a word!

"Will you cherish and preserve this life-stone?" repeated Hamul-Kammesh, still displaying the ornament.

But still she could not reply. Her shoulders twitched, and a shudder ran through her body; her lips trembled, but not a sound came forth.

"For the third time," repeated the soothsayer, in impressive tones, "I ask whether you wish the life-stone? You are not compelled to answer, but unless you do answer you cannot be married. If for the third time you fail to reply, your silence will mean refusal, and there must be no further festivities today; but the guests must leave, and no suitor must seek your favor for another year. And so for the last time I put the question—"

"Yes, yes, give me the life-stone!" sighed Yasma, in a broken voice, as she reached toward the red trifle.

Without delay, Hamul-Kammesh hung the symbol of our union about her neck.

As soon as Yasma and I had received our life-stones, the "sacru" was passed and became the center of attention. The occasion was more than welcome to me, not because of the liquor, which I scarcely tasted, but for the sake of Yasma, with whom I desired an occasional word on this our bridal day. While the men and women were crowding forward for their share of the drink, I recognized my opportunity; and, motioning Yasma to follow me, I threaded my way to the edge of the crowd and beyond the furthest cabin to a trail winding through the woods. Fortunately, no one seemed to notice our departure, for the enchantment of the "sacru" was already at work.

Yasma seemed glad enough to accompany me; but though she shared in my relief at breaking free from the crowd, her conduct was still peculiar. She did not show any of the happiness natural to a bride, but was moody and sad. She answered my questions and remarks only with monosyllables, yet was by no means cold or indifferent, and gave evidence of her affection by the clinging closeness with which she held my arm.

Having reached the woods, we seated ourselves side by side on a log at the borders of some fragrant white-flowering bushes; and there we began our wedded life in an unlooked-for fashion.

"Well, Yasma, we have come to the end of our separate roads," I reminded her, patting her hand and trying to conceal my anxiety. "From now on we shall follow one path together. Surely, it shall always make us happy to look back upon this day. Shall it not, Yasma?"

Yasma's response was far from reassuring. A long silence intervened, while she sat with head bent low and eyes averted. Suddenly, as I sought to draw her close, I became aware that her whole form was quivering.

"Yasma!" I cried, dismayed and bewildered, as I took the weeping girl into my arms. "Yasma, Yasma dear, what is wrong?"

"Oh, I'm so afraid, so afraid!" she wailed, as she clung to me, her face still turned away. "Please, please take good care of me! I'm so afraid—I don't know why—I can't help it!"

Almost desperately she held me, and buried her face against my breast, and sobbed and sobbed while I strove in vain to console her.

"But what can be the matter, Yasma?" I asked, beseechingly, when the storm was beginning to spend itself. "I don't understand—I don't understand at all!"

"Oh, I don't understand, either!" she burst forth, vehemently. "It's silly of me, simply silly! There's no reason, not the least! Oh, you shouldn't care for me, you shouldn't, you shouldn't!"

And the tears came in a renewed torrent, and it was minutes before they had subsided again.

"Don't pay any attention to me—I'm too foolish!" she murmured, as she sat clinging to me, her face still pitifully moist. "I know I shouldn't act like this, but everything seems so strange and new. And I keep thinking that what we've done today can never be taken back, never, never! That thought frightens me. What if—what if Yulada should still be angry with us?"

Of course, I strove my best to soothe away her fears. I told her that we had nothing to dread from Yulada; that we had acted wisely and should always be glad of it. Yet, even as I spoke, I could not be convinced of the truth of my own words. And I am afraid that I did not convince her. For she cut me short with an outburst such as I had not expected even from her.

"Oh, let's forget Yulada—forget everything! Forget everything but you and me! Nothing, nothing else can matter! I have you, and that is all I want. That is all I ever want! Oh, stay with me, stay with me, my beloved, and I do not care what Yulada may do—no, I do not care what may happen in the whole world!"

Her words ended in another sobbing crescendo; but this time it was not so hard to console her. Soon, calmed by my coaxing, she dried her tears, and looked up into my face, timidly smiling; and at this I forgot all my misgivings, and told her how blessed she was making me; and she answered with a coy tossing of the head, and murmured things that my memory will treasure always but that may not be repeated.

It was almost dusk when we returned to the village. From afar we could hear the shouts and cries of the revelers, the booming of drums, the shrilling of horns; and, upon approaching, we found the people riotously absorbed in their games. Some were engaged in feats of wrestling and jumping; some were racing about after little wooden balls; some were juggling with pebbles, and some twisting their bodies into fantastic contortions; some were dancing in a long writhing serpentine; some scuttled to and fro like children in games of hide-and-seek; some staggered aimlessly hither and thither with the weight of too much "sacru."

So preoccupied were the people that our return was scarcely noted; indeed, it was not apparent that our absence had even been observed. But we did not care; we were glad enough to be left alone; and, after satisfying our hunger from the fruits and dainties being passed about on wooden platters, we withdrew to a secluded corner to await the firelight festivities. Gladly we would have left entirely; but we must be present later in the evening, when, in the midst of the cheering, congratulatory throng, we would be escorted to my cabin, which had been bedecked with ribbons and equipped with household supplies by our friends, and which would be the stage for a second and briefer ceremony under the auspices of Hamul-Kammesh.

But before that ceremony could take place, there was to be an unscheduled exhibition. The sunset fires had barely died and the bright yellow full moon peeped above the eastern ranges, when an uncanny ruddy light flared beneath the moon; a great ball of fire blazed into sight, soaring high with startling swiftness, like a projectile shot out of some colossal gun. Sultry red with a glare that drowned out the luster of the moon and stars, it went hurtling in a long curve across the heavens and beyond the western peaks; and as it swept out of view, sputtering and scintillating like a burning rocket, an unearthly hissing came to our ears;

while, after the specter had retreated, a long copper furrow remained to mark its pathway, glowing and smoldering and only gradually fading out amid the thin starlight.

The effect upon the Ibandru was overpowering. Within a few seconds the celestial visitant had flashed into life and vanished; but for hours the wedding guests could only gape and stare, muttering in alarm, walking about as if distracted, prostrating themselves upon the ground and praying to Yulada. All merrymaking was over for the night; no one even thought of further festivities. "A portent! A portent!" cried the people; and no words of mine could dissuade them. Useless to tell them that they had observed merely a great meteor,—they were convinced that Yulada had sent them a message, a warning; convinced that my marriage was an unhallowed thing, and that only misfortune could follow. Even Yasma shared in the general panic; her fears of a few hours before were revived; and as she huddled against me, huddled desperately as a child in need of comfort, I could feel her whole body quaking; and I had the impression that I was holding not a woman but a caged bird suddenly conscious of its bars.

CHAPTER XVIII
THE SECOND FLIGHT BEGINS

Whenever I recall my sorrows and misfortunes in Sobul, I am tormented also by happy memories that wound like fresh trials. And foremost among those memories I place my first few months with Yasma. If a cloud hovered over our betrothal and a deeper cloud descended upon our marriage day, the skies became immediately blue again once the wedding festival was over. The consternation produced in Yasma's mind by the meteor proved to be only temporary; if she ever remembered it again, she did not mention the fact; and if she had any remaining scruples regarding Yulada and the righteousness of our marriage, she kept her doubts to herself. To me she was all sweetness, kindness and devotion; a new radiance seemed to have overspread her countenance, and her face shone with a richer and more beautiful light than ever; while all her movements were imbued with the grace and airiness of one at once perfectly carefree and perfectly unspoiled.

So potently had Yasma woven her spell over me that for the time I was a convert to the ways of Sobul. As the Ibandru lived, so I lived; momentarily I had almost forgotten that I was the son of civilized lands. Each morning I would go forth with Karem and Barkodu to till the fields; and each noon and evening I would return to a home where skilled feminine hands had prepared a tasteful meal. Sometimes, when the work on the farms was not too pressing, I would join the tribesmen in day-long expeditions across the mountains, expeditions in which Yasma would always take part; sometimes there would be holidays when I would go fishing with Karem or roaming the woods with Yasma; and in the evenings, except in the infrequent event of rain, I would take part with the others in the village sports, running and wrestling, dancing and singing, competing in the games, or merely sitting about the campfire exchanging reminiscences.

Now at last I was accepted almost as a native of Sobul. My marriage to a daughter of the tribe apparently made the people think of me as an Ibandru by adoption; yes, even though in some ways I was still a stranger, and though the people still were silent when I questioned them as to their autumnal flight. If any of them recalled Hamul-Kammesh's original prophecy, and in particular the omen of the fireball, they were careful to keep their recollections quiet; and even if they had their fears, they cherished no personal resentment—for was it not Yulada herself who had showed me the way to Sobul? Was it not by her will that I was remaining?

Certainly, it seemed to suit the pleasure of Yulada that I should linger here indefinitely. The way to the outer world was still unknown; no visitors came to Sobul, and in my wanderings among the mountains I had discovered no sign of human life and no road that gave promise of leading toward civilization. Not that I would have left if I could; to go away without Yasma would have been unthinkable; and to go with her would have been as difficult as it was dangerous. Yet I kept wondering if I was to spend my remaining days in this primitive valley; and I had more than an occasional day-dream of finding some previously unobserved mountain pass and making my way with Yasma toward some civilized settlement.

But as yet, in the happiness of my young wedded life, such thoughts troubled me very little. No one in my country was half so dear to me as Yasma; and all the friends I had left, the habits I had abandoned and the work I had lost could not weigh in the scales against her. And so for a while I merely toyed with the thought of escape; and even had it seemed possible to extricate myself from the wilderness of Sobul, I should scarcely have stirred to make the attempt. Months passed, and all remained as it had been; the hot days came, and the woods were densely green again with the summer foliage; the fruit of the orchards swelled and ripened, the plum was dyed a rich purple, and the face of the peach was delicately pink. But Yasma and I, in our enchanted retreat, scarcely noted the passing of the weeks, scarcely were aware that we were drifting on a slow tide toward the end of bliss. At times, indeed, some prematurely yellowing leaf or some field newly prepared for the harvest, would bring an uncomfortable premonition of autumn; at times the sight of Yulada perched inscrutably upon the peak would awaken unpleasant reminders of the past winter and still more unpleasant reminders of the winter to come. But mostly I managed to thrust such thoughts from me, to live in the enjoyment of the present moment, and to feel that the present moment was to endure. I was only deceiving myself with phantoms!—alas, I did not succeed in deceiving myself completely!— and now and then, when the veil was momentarily lifted, I was aware that a shadow still brooded above me, that for the moment it was dim and far-away, but that it would return, return as certainly as the days would grow frosty and the birds fly south once more!

I had been in Sobul more than a year when my worst forebodings seemed about to be fulfilled. The days were again on their decline; the unharvested fields once more lay ripe before the reaper; a chill began to creep into the air of evenings, and the landscape was occasionally blurred with mist; the wild fruits and nuts were falling in the forest, and the squirrels were laying up their winter supplies; the woods began to take on a ragged lining of brown and yellow and premature golden, and more than an occasional leaf was fluttering down in early deference to the fall.

Then came October; and with October I grew aware, as a year before, of an undercurrent of excitement in the village. Once more the youths and maidens had seemingly lost interest in their noisy evening pastimes; once more the people were growing restless and uneasy; once more they bore the aspect of waiting, of waiting for some imminent and momentous event.

Even Yasma did not escape the general anxiety. At times I observed a far-away look in her eyes, a melancholy that I could not quite fathom; and at such moments she would seek to avoid my presence. At other times she would burst without apparent cause into fits of weeping, and would cling to me, and beg me to forgive her if she could not do her duty and were not a good wife. But always it seemed futile to question her; for did I not surmise what the trouble was? Could I forget that the season of cold winds was at hand?

Not until the first southward flight of the birds did my fears crystallize. It was as if this event, the occasion for wild rejoicing among the Ibandru, signalized the close of my idyllic life with Yasma. On a day of wind and gathering cloud, when the first triangle of living dots came soaring from across the mountains and out of sight beyond Yulada, it seemed as if the birds were speeding away with my hopes. Just as a year before, the entire village became tumultuously excited, and abandoned all other occupations to watch the winged travelers; and, as a year before, a great firelight celebration was held, in which all the tribe participated, and over which Abthar and Hamul-Kammesh presided.

But although the ceremonies of a year ago were almost duplicated, I did not find this festival so interesting as the former. Rather, I found it terrifying, for it brought me visions of deserted cabins and snow-clad mountainsides, and seemed to impose a dismal gulf between Yasma and me.

To reassure myself, I sought to stay at Yasma's side during the celebration. But somehow she slipped away, much as last year; and I could find no trace of her until late that night I discovered her in our cabin with moist face, and eyes that even by the flickering firelight seemed swollen and red.

"Yasma!" I cried. "What is the matter?"

For a moment she did not reply, but looked at me with large smoldering eyes. Then tenderly she came to me, placed her hands upon my shoulders, and murmured, "I was thinking of you, my beloved, thinking of you here all alone when the cold winds blow and the days grow gray and empty, and there is no one, no one to take care of you!"

Overcome by her own words, she gave way to sobbing.

And I, faced with the inevitable, could only put the question I had put so many times before. "But could you not stay with me here, Yasma? Could you not—"

"No, no, no!" she interrupted, in the midst of her tears. "I could not, could not! Yulada would not permit it!"

"Not even for me?" I entreated, as one might entreat a favor of a refractory child.

"Not even for you! Could I make my heart stop beating for you? Could I cease breathing and still live because you wished it of me? No, no, no, do not ask me to change my nature!"

"I would not ask you to change your nature, Yasma," I assured her gently, as I took her again into my arms. "But I love you so much, my dearest, so much that I can hardly bear to think of being parted from you."

"Or I to be parted from you!"

Mastered once more by her emotion, she turned from me, wringing her hands.

A long, silent moment intervened before she faced me again. But when she did turn to me, her face was more composed, and her eyes shone with new resolution.

"Let us try to be brave, my beloved," she urged. "I will stay with you here a while yet; will stay as long as Yulada permits. And what if, after I go, the winter must come?—it will pass, and the green leaves will grow again, and the snow will melt on the mountainsides; and I will come back, come back with the first northward-flying birds!"

She paused, and smiled in melancholy reassurance. But I did not reply, and the smile quickly faded; and she continued, pleadingly, "Remember, my beloved, when you asked me to marry you, you said you were willing to lose me half the year. You promised, or I could never have consented. So why are you not willing now?"

"Yes, I did promise," I admitted, with a groan. "I did promise, and I know I should be willing. But how different things seemed then! How much harder to lose you after all these months together! Why, Yasma, I must lose you without even knowing where you're going! At least, you might tell me that! How would you feel if I went away and you didn't know where?"

As always before, my pleas had no effect except to bring the tears to Yasma's eyes.

"Do you not think I would tell you if I could?" she asked, gently and sadly. "But Yulada would not permit it, and I dare not lift my voice against her. I could not if I would. For there are things we cannot describe, and things that can be known only to those that share in them. Could you expect the wild dove to tell you of its flight? Could you expect the eagle to make known the joy it feels when it sails into the sun?"

"Oh, but you are not as the eagle or the dove!" I protested.

"Why do you think we are not?" she returned, with a curious smile.

At this query I was struck by a fancy so wild that even now I hesitate to mention it: the thought that Yasma and her people were not wholly human! that for half the year they walked the earth as men and women, and for the other half sailed the sky as birds! Nor did this notion seem quite so absurd as it would have appeared before my arrival in Sobul. Here in this world-forsaken valley, with its periodically migrating inhabitants, anything at all seemed possible; even the supernatural appeared to lose its remote and fabulous glow. And so, for an instant, I had the impression that something unearthly enveloped Yasma, even Yasma, my wife! And once again, as on first coming to Sobul, I experienced the sense of other-worldly forces at work all about me, forces that had Yasma in their keeping and were bound to wrest her from me, no matter how I might groan and struggle, no matter how I might cry out and entreat and reach forth my arms and call and call after her dwindling form!

CHAPTER XIX
THE CYCLE IS COMPLETED

With what sadness I watched the autumn gradually return to Sobul! The crimson and tan and russet woods, glowing with a forlorn and dying inner radiance, were tragic as with the sorrow of a crumbling universe; each frightened leaf that scurried earthward with a sharp blast, seemed laden with some hope that had withered; the legions of wild ducks and geese that went speeding ever, ever beyond the southern peaks, were to me awe-inspiring and solemn portents. And the clouds that came whirling and clustering by in troops and squadrons at the goad of the high wind, were grim with evil reminders; and their glee in overrunning the sky's blue and blurring the fringes of the peaks, was as the glee of those dark forces that invisibly blotted out my happiness.

Partly in order to drive tormenting premonitions from my mind, I tried to keep well occupied during those harrowing days. I had not forgotten the preparations I had made for the previous winter, nor the need of fortifying myself for the winter to come. Once again I gathered large supplies of food and firewood; once again I sealed all cracks and crannies in my cabin walls, procured heavy garments, and made ready for a hermit's life. And in these preparations Yasma helped me as energetically and skillfully as last year. But she worked sadly, and in silence; and often the tears were in her eyes as she stored the firewood in orderly heaps or arranged the dried fruits, nuts and grains in neat and convenient piles.

I alone, just as last autumn, was preparing for the winter; as time went by, the other inhabitants of Sobul were going their mute and mysterious way. Gradually the village was being deserted; face after familiar face was disappearing: first Abthar, then Barkodu, then Karem, then Hamul-Kammesh; while by degrees the town assumed a desolate appearance. The end of October saw its population reduced by more than half; early November found a mere handful remaining; and I knew that the time was not far-off when even this handful would have vanished. But where the people went was as much an enigma as ever.

As during the previous year, I made several attempts to trace the fugitives. More than once, slipping out of the cabin at night when Yasma was asleep, I lay in wait for hours in a thicket at the village edge; but my only reward was fresh torment and bewilderment. I never caught any glimpse of the departing natives, though always in the morning I would note that there were more absentees; on my most successful attempt, I found a number of fresh-made tracks, which I hopefully traced southward into the woods, until they came to an end as inexplicably as though their makers had evaporated.

I well remember my last effort. I must have been a little incautious in leaving the cabin; or perhaps Yasma was not quite asleep, as I had thought; for no sooner had I taken my usual station in the thicket than I became aware of a shadowy approaching form. Thinking that this was one of the fleeing Ibandru, I crouched down so as not to be seen; but a peal of laughter brought me to my senses; in an instant, I found myself face to face with—my wife!

"Oh, you silly creature, how do you expect to find out anything that way?" she chided me, having apparently divined my purpose. "You may lie there watching till the end of time, and you'll never discover a thing. It is not by examining the earth that you may learn of the eagle's flight."

With these words Yasma took my arm; and docilely I accompanied her back to our cabin.

Only by a great effort of will had I dared to leave her side that night, for I lived in terror that when I next turned to look for her she would be gone. Indeed, if she had been a bubble that might burst at a touch, or a rainbow that a shadow would shatter, I could scarcely have been more worried; for it would hardly have surprised me to see her transform herself into a sun-mote, and go dancing into the air and out of view.

November was not yet very old when some persistent voice within me proclaimed that the crisis was at hand. There arrived a day when not a score of the Ibandru paced about among the empty cabins; there arrived a later day when not half a score were to be seen, and then the climactic day—not very much later—when only one member of the tribe still walked in the village.

Even at this distant hour I can relive the sorrow and passion of that day. I remember how the solemn gray clouds went scudding beneath the gray solemn sky; how the wild geese, the last of the winged migrants, called and called plaintively on their way southward; how the wind, like a harried soul that answered the driven birds, shrieked and wailed when its impetuous gusts chased down the last of the red leaves and scattered the swirling eddies of dust. A wild, mad day! a day when the whole earth seemed risen in fury and revolt! a day when the elements, alive with the vehemence and vain frenzy of all created things, were voicing the sadness and despair of the universe in a dirge for the dying year!

And on that tumultuous day, in that world of raging wind and cloud, Yasma came to me with such a light in her eyes as the dying may show when they bid farewell to love. One glance at her shuddering form confirmed my fears; I knew her message, and felt intuitively the hopelessness of protest or reproach.

Without a word she flung her arms about me, stormily sobbing; and I held her in an embrace so long and fierce that I might have been a foe striving to crush her frail body.

But at length she struggled free, and stood before me, moist-eyed and pathetically smiling. "Good-bye, my beloved, good-bye," she murmured, and edged toward the door.

"Do not go, do not go!" I cried, and I stretched out my arms imploringly. But some numbing force had paralyzed my limbs—I was unable to move a step.

"Good-bye, my beloved," she repeated, with a look like a tormented angel's. "Good-bye—until the spring!"

And her slender form slipped past the door, and its wooden bulk closed behind her. And as she escaped, sudden action came to my frozen limbs, and I rushed out of the cabin, calling and calling, "Yasma! Yasma!" And then, frantically, "Yasma! Yasma!" But only the wind replied. A whirl of dust struck me in the face, and for a moment I was half blinded. Then, when I turned to look for Yasma, no Yasma was to be seen. And in bewilderment and balked anger and despair, I realized that I should see her no more until the birds were flying north.

III
THE WILL OF YULADA

CHAPTER XX
THE SECOND WINTER

It would be pointless to dwell at length upon my second winter in Sobul. In everything essential, it was a repetition of the winter before. There were the same long solitary months, the same monotonous loneliness by the evening firelight, the same trudging through the snow on companionless expeditions, the same arduous gathering of faggots and the same fear of predatory wild things, the same howling of wolves from across the valley and the same clamoring of storm-winds, the same bleak questionings and the same impotent wrath at the unkindliness of my fate.

But in one respect my lot this year was harder to bear. For now there were memories to torment, memories that arose like ghosts when in the long evenings I sat musing by the golden-yellow light of the log blaze. A year ago there had also been memories; a year ago I had also thought of Yasma with sadness; but then there had been no endearing intimacy to haunt every object she had brightened with her presence and every spot her feet had pressed. Now the very cabin she had occupied with me seemed desolate because she had been there; the very pans and kettles and earthen vessels her fingers had touched became sorrowful reminders, while a little spray of wildflowers, gathered by her hands months before and now hanging gray and withered from the log wall, was the perpetual source of longing and regret. How strange and ironic that every gay moment we had passed together should have its melancholy echoes, and that her very smiles and laughter and little winning ways and little loving kindnesses should all return to mock me now!

As I sat dreaming of Yasma, my thoughts would flicker fitfully as the flames writhing in the fireplace. One moment I would blame myself for bringing misfortune upon my beloved; the next moment anger would rise in my heart and I would feel aggrieved at her and at the world because I had been forsaken. And when I remembered that this second lonely winter might not be the last, that next winter and every winter I might be deserted, then a furious resolve blazed up within me; and with a strength born of my wretchedness I determined that never again should I live through the cold season alone. Let Yasma refuse to stay, and I would coax, cajole, entreat, and if need be force her to remain. Was she not my wife? Was it not unreasonable to be abandoned as she had abandoned me? No doubt she would plead that she had never promised to stay, had always insisted on the need for a migration—but might that need not be a mere superstition, born of blind obedience to some secret tribal tradition? And, whatever the necessity that moved her, how could it compare with my own necessity?

Another winter of solitary confinement, I feared, and I should go mad. Already I was tending toward the obsessions that beset one overlong in his own company—and should I do Yasma a favor by bequeathing her a lunatic for a husband? Plainly, she did not understand, could not understand, any more than I could understand her ways; but was it not my duty to protect us both by any means within my grasp? Thus I reasoned, repeating the arguments over and over to myself, until I knew them as the mathematician knows his axioms; and so, partly by logic and partly by sophistry and largely because of the frenzy of my love and despair, I decided upon that step which was to make all succeeding winters different, and was to mark the fateful climax of my life in Sobul.

Having made my resolve, I could face the world with fresh courage. All that winter, when the mountains were white specters beneath the blue sky or when the clouds blotted out the peaks and the snow was sifted down day after day, I kept hope alive not only at the thought of Yasma's return in the spring but by the determination that she should not leave in the autumn. I might be tormented by loneliness; I might read only sorrow in the denuded woods, and menace in the lowering skies; I might quiver at the wail of the wolf, and people the shadows of the night with evil shapes; I might find the peaks cruelly aloof, and Yulada as disdainful as ever on her rock-throne; yet at least I had something to clutch at, something to bring me consolation and make it seem worth while to live.

But there was another thought that lent the world interest. Yulada still drew me toward her with a mysterious fascination; I was as anxious as ever to climb to her feet. My previous failures did not discourage me; I told myself that I had been unlucky, and should succeed if I persisted. Had the upper altitudes not been coated with ice, I should have made the attempt immediately after Yasma's departure; but experience had taught me to wait; and I determined that early in the spring, before the first Ibandru had reappeared, I should again match my strength with the elusive slopes.

It was when March was still young that a benign mildness came into the air; that the snow began to melt, and the streams to run full to the brim. During most of the month the warmth endured; and shortly before the arrival of April the peaks were banded and mottled with wide gray patches, and I concluded that it was time for my new adventure.

I was not at fault in this judgment. Never before had the ascent seemed quite so easy; the way had been smoothed as though by invisible hands. No ice or snow impeded me along the lower slopes, or blockaded me on the upper; no impassable cliff intervened as I followed the windings of the trail through groves of deodar and pine, and along the verge of thousand-foot precipices. But the blue sky, the invigorating breezes and the new-washed glittering peaks all served to strengthen my determination. To climb to Yulada appeared almost a simple matter, and I could scarcely understand why I had not succeeded before.

Yet somehow I could not remain cheerful as the hours went by and I trudged along the stony ledges and over ridge after steep projecting ridge. Or was I being infected with the same superstition as the Ibandru felt?

This much, at least, I know: the higher I mounted, the lower my spirits sank; I began to feel as one who sacrilegiously invades a shrine; had I not opposed my determination to my fears, I might not have come within miles of Yulada.

But, after several hours, my stubbornness appeared to be winning. By early afternoon I had mounted high among the bare ridges at Yulada's feet; the stone figure loomed not many hundred yards above, proud and defiant as ever, so huge that she could have held me like a pebble in one hand, and so majestic that she seemed the masterpiece of some titanic artist. Truly, an awe-inspiring, a terrifying sight! Truly, I had reason to feel my own insignificance as I stood gazing at those cyclopean outlines, the steel-gray contours of the exquisitely modelled figure, the firm and haughty face inexorably set like the face of fate itself, the hands upraised as though in supplication to the Unseen, and one foot lifted as if to step into the abyss.

If I had been sanguine before, I was now merely appalled. It seemed impossible that I, a pygmy intruder, should ever stand within touching distance of the goddess! Surely some sign would come, as always before, to checkmate my approach; either the fog would rise, or the storms be hatched, or my feet would falter and fall. So I thought as with painstaking slowness I attacked the final few hundred yards, watching every step and half expecting the ground to give way or the earth itself to open.

With vigorous efforts, the last lap might have been accomplished in half an hour; but my cautious crawl took nearer to an hour and a half. During all that time I had scarcely a glimpse of Yulada, for the grade was such that I could observe her only as the pedestrian at the base of a skyscraper may view the flagpole. Yet I was so busy creeping on hands and knees up the steep inclines, that I could give Yulada hardly a thought. I did not doubt that, having mastered the slopes, I should be able to inspect the goddess to advantage.

Finally, in joy not unmixed with dread, I was reaching the end of my climb. One last pinnacle to surmount, and I should stand face to face with Yulada! I could scarcely believe in my own good fortune—would the rock not crumble beneath me, and hurl me into the void? But no! the rock was solid enough; with one climactic effort, I lifted myself over the brink, and stood safely on the peak!

But was I on the peak? What was that irregular gray mass above? I blinked, and observed that I was on a narrow plateau, over which there loomed a great pile of crags, jagged and beetling and apparently without form or design. For a moment I stared in idiotic bewilderment; then gradual recognition came to me. This shapeless heap of rock was Yulada! It was only from a distance that her outlines appeared human; seen at close range, she was but a fantastic formation of stone!

In my first surprise and disappointment at the irony of the discovery, I laughed aloud. Yet I was not slow to understand. I remembered how a fine painting, splendid at several yards, may seem a blur to one who approaches too closely. And was Yulada not a masterwork of nature, intended for inspection only from afar? Her form, as I saw it, was full of flaws and irregularities, but how well distance smoothed away the defects, supplying her with statuesque outlines that were unreal, a verisimilitude that was only illusion!

For almost an hour I lingered at Yulada's feet, trying to penetrate what still remained of her secret. But there seemed little enough to penetrate. The rugged granite of her body, scarred and polished by the tempests of centuries, was responsible for her gray color; her head, neck, face and limbs were barely distinguishable—she was as any other crag which nature, chance sculptress, had modelled into something lifelike and rare.

As I strolled about the base of Yulada, I found myself wondering about the beliefs of the Ibandru, their dread of approaching the stone figure. And suddenly an explanation came to me. What if some wily priest, climbing long ago where I had climbed today, had realized that his power would be enhanced and the fear of Yulada intensified if the people were never to ascend to the peak? And what if, having conspired with his fellow priests, he had passed an edict forbidding his followers, under dire penalties, to mount within five stones' throws of the statue-like figure? Among a superstitious people, could not such a taboo be made impressive?

But though my reason accepted this explanation, I am an inconsistent individual, and my emotions rejected it utterly. Even as I stood gazing up at the rocky mass, fear crept back into my heart; irrational questionings forced themselves once more upon me despite all that good sense could do to keep them out. Were the Ibandru wholly at fault in dreading Yulada? in dreading to stand at her feet? Here again it may have been only my imagination at work; but when a cloud came drifting out of nowhere across the sky and for a moment dimmed the sun, I had a sense of some mysterious overshadowing presence. And all at once I was anxious to escape, to free myself from the uncanny imminence of the peak; and it seemed that the great stone mass above, and the cloud-flecked sky, and the billowy gaunt ranges, were all joined against me in some gigantic conspiracy.

As rapidly as safety permitted, I made my way down from the mountain. But still strange fears disturbed me, that same inexplicable uneasiness which had obsessed me so often in Sobul. Heedless of hunger and fatigue, sore muscles and blistered feet, I continued downward for hours; and that evening I made camp between two sheltered crags just above the timber-line.

Yet the day's torments were not over. As I skilfully struck my two flints to make a fire, a greater and more arresting fire was flaring in the west. Huge masses of cloud were heaped above the dark ranges, and to the east the bars and patches of snow were smoldering with a mellow rose-red. But their light was dim beside that of the clouds, which were luminously golden, as though great flames leapt and sparkled in their heart; and above the clouds the crimson of the sky was such as may overtop the towers of a burning city. Spellbound, I watched; and, as I watched, the crimson seemed gradually to take form; and the shape was at first vague and indistinguishable, but by degrees became more clearly pencilled; and then, perhaps owing to the downward drift of the clouds, and perhaps because my imagination endowed the scene with unreal qualities, I thought that I could make out a face, a red peering face as vast as a mountain! And that face had familiar outlines; and in amazement and horror and dismay I recognized the features—of Yulada!

For one moment only, the hallucination endured; then the countenance became blurred and unrecognizable, and the crimson was drowned out by the gray, and the fierce blaze of sunset was quenched and subdued, and the twilight deepened, and the stars came out. But all that night, while the constellations gleamed above and I lay huddled close to my fire, I could not sleep but restlessly stirred from side to side, for I kept seeing over and over again that terrible vision of Yulada.

CHAPTER XXI
THE MOLEB

When at last I saw the green leaves unfolding on the trees, the green grass springing up in every meadow and the orchards bursting into flower, my hopes and fears of the year before were revived. Daily I watched for the Ibandru's return; daily I was divided between expectation and dread. How be sure that they would come back at all? How be certain that, even if they did reappear, Yasma would be among them?

But my fears were not to be realized. There came an April day when I rejoiced to see Karem and a fellow tribesman emerging from the southern woods; there came a day when I was reunited to one dearer to me than Karem. From the first men to return I had received vague tidings of Yasma, being told that she was well and would be back soon; but my anxiety did not cease until I had actually seen her.

Our second reunion was similar in most ways to our first. Awakening at dawn when the first pale light was flowing in through the open window, I was enchanted to hear the trill of a bird-song, tremulous and ethereally sweet, the love-call of some unknown melodist to its mate. Somewhere, I remembered, I had been charmed by such a song before, for it had a quality all its own, a richness and plaintiveness that made it unforgettable. At first I could not recall when I had heard that sound, if in my own country or here in Sobul; then, as I lay listening in a pleasant revery, recognition came to me. It was precisely such a song that had captivated me a year ago just before Yasma's return!

As I made this discovery, the song suddenly ended. Hopefully I staggered up from my couch; for a moment I stood peering through the window in a trance. Then there came a light tapping at the door. My heart gave a flutter; I was scarcely able to cry out, "Come in!"

Slowly the door began to turn inward, creaking and groaning with its reluctant motion. But I ran to it and wrenched it wide open, and there Yasma stood, staring me in the face!

She seemed as much overjoyed as was I, and our greeting was such as only sundered lovers can know.

Several minutes passed before I could look at her closely. Then, freeing myself from her embrace, I observed that she was unchanged—the same vivid, buoyant creature as always! Her eyes could still dance merrily, her cheeks were still aglow with health; even her clothes were unaltered, for she wore the same crimson and blue garments as when she left, and they appeared hardly the worse for wear.

But, even as last year, she noticed a change in me.

"You look thinner and more worn, my beloved," she remarked, sadly, as she stood scrutinizing me with tender concern. "You look like one who has been ill. Have you actually been unwell?"

I replied that I had not been unwell—why tell her that my one affliction had been her absence?

But now that she was back, I was willing to cast aside all bleak remembrances. I was as one awakened from a nightmare; I was so thankful that I could have leapt and shouted like a schoolboy. All that day, I could scarcely trust myself out of sight of her, so fearful was I that I might find her vanished; and she would scarcely trust herself out of sight of me, so delighted was she at having returned. I am afraid that we both behaved a little like children; but if our conduct was a trifle foolish, it was at least very pleasant.

Nevertheless, a shadow hovered all the while beside us. Most of the time, it was not visible, but it swung across our path whenever I mentioned Yasma's winter absence or sought to discover where she had been hiding. As always before, she was sphinx-like on this subject; and since I had no desire to ruin our first day's happiness, I was cautious to bring up the matter only casually. Yet I assured myself that I should have no such question to ask next spring.

During the following days, as the Ibandru gradually returned and the village began to take on an inhabited appearance, I tried to forget the mystery that still brooded about us, and cheerfully resumed my last year's activities, almost as if there had been no interruption. More days than not I worked in the fields with the other men; occasionally Yasma and her kindred accompanied me on the mountain trails, exploring many a splintered ridge and deeply sunken gorge; in the evening I would sit with the tribesmen around the communal fire, exchanging anecdotes and describing over and over again my far-off, almost dreamy-dim life in my own land.

And once again Yasma and I were happy. The glamour of our first few wedded months was revived; we had almost forgotten that the glow could ever fade, scarcely remembered the old omens and predictions; and if any of the villagers ever muttered their secret fears, they made sure that we were well out of hearing. Yet all the while I realized that we were living in a house of glass, and Yasma must have realized it too; and in bad dreams at times I heard the rumbling of approaching storms, and saw the fragile walls of paradise come clattering about our feet in ruins.

Only one notable event occurred between the return of the Ibandru and the flight of the first birds southward. And that was an event I had awaited for two years, and would once have welcomed fervently. As it happened, it had little immediate effect; but it broke rocket-like upon my tranquillity, awakened long-slumbering desires, and brought me bright and vivid visions of the world I had lost.

It was in mid-July that I took an unexpectedly interesting expedition among the mountains. Yasma accompanied me, as always; Karem and Barkodu and a dozen other natives completed the party. We were to carry copious provisions, were to venture further into the wilderness than I had ever penetrated before, and were not to return in less than three days, for we intended to journey to a snowy western peak where grew a potent herb, "the moleb," which Hamul-Kammesh recommended as a sure cure for all distempers of the mind and body.

No other mountaineering expedition had ever given me so much pleasure. Truly, the "moleb" did have remarkable qualities; even before we had gathered the first spray of this little weed my lungs were filled with the exhilaration of the high mountain air, and all my distempers of the mind and body had been cured. I breathed of the free cool breezes of the peaks, and felt how puny was the life I had once led among brick walls; I stood gazing into the vacancies of dim, deep canyons, and through blue miles to the shoulders of remote cloud-wrapped ranges, and it seemed to me that I was king and master of all this tumultuous expanse of green and brown and azure. The scenery was magnificent; the sharply cloven valleys, the snow-streaked summits and wide dark-green forests stretched before me even as they may have stretched before my paleolithic forebears; and nowhere was there a funnel of smoke, or a hut or shanty, or a devastated woodland to serve as the signature of man.

Yet amid these very solitudes, where all things human appeared as remote as some other planet, I was to find my first hint of the way back to civilized lands. It was afternoon of the second day, and we had gathered a supply of the "moleb" and were returning to Sobul, when I beheld a sight that made me stare as if in a daze. Far, far beneath us, slowly threading their way toward the top of the rocky ridge we were descending, were half a dozen steadily moving black dots!

In swift excitement, I turned to Karem and Barkodu, and asked who these men might be. But my companions appeared unconcerned; they remarked that the strangers were doubtless natives of these regions; and they advised that we allow them to pass without seeing us, for the country was infested with brigands.

But brigands or no brigands, I was determined to talk with the newcomers. All the pleas of Yasma and the arguments of Karem were powerless to move me. I had a dim hope that the strangers might be of my own race; and a stronger hope that they could give me welcome news. At all events, they were the first human beings other than the Ibandru that I had seen for two years, and the opportunity was not one to scorn.

As there was only one trail up the steep, narrow slope, the unknowns would have to pass us unless we hid. And since I would not hide and my companions would not desert me, it was not long before the strangers had hailed us. Up and up they plodded in long snaky curves, now lost from view beyond a ledge, now reappearing from behind some great crag; while gradually they became more clearly outlined. It was not long before we had made out that their garments were of a gray unlike anything worn in Sobul; and at about the same time we began to distinguish something of their faces, which were covered with black beards.

As yet my companions had not overcome the suspicion that we were thrusting ourselves into the hands of bandits. But when we came close we found that the strangers, while stern-browed and flashing-eyed, and not of the type that one would carelessly antagonize, were amiably disposed. At a glance, I recognized their kinship to those guides who, two years before, had led our geological party into this country. Their bearing was resolute, almost martial; their well formed features were markedly aquiline; their hair, after the fashion of the land, was shaved off to the top of the head, and at the sides it fell in long curls that reached the shoulders.

Gravely they greeted us in the Pushtu tongue; and gravely we returned their salutation. But their accent was not that of the Ibandru; often my comrades and I had difficulty in making out their phrases; while they in turn were puzzled at much that we said. None the less, we managed to get along tolerably well.

They came from a town a day's travel to westward, they announced; and had been visiting some friends in the valley beneath, only a quarter of a day's journey to the southeast. They were surprised to see us, since travelers were not often encountered among these mountains; but their delight equalled their surprise, for they should like to call us their friends, and perhaps, if our homes were not too far-off, they should sometime visit us.

It was obvious that they had never seen any of our kind before, nor any blue and red costumes like ours. But I was not pleased to find myself the particular object of attention. From the first, the strangers were staring at me curiously, somewhat as one stares at a peculiar new animal.

As long as I could, I endured their scrutiny; then, when it seemed as if they would never withdraw their gaze, my annoyance found words.

"Maybe you wouldn't mind telling me," I asked, "why you all keep looking at me so oddly? Do you find anything unusual about me?"

None of the strangers seemed surprised at the question. "No, I wouldn't mind telling you," declared one who appeared to be their leader. "We do find something unusual about you. You are wearing the same sort of clothes as your friends, who were surely born in the mountains; but it is clear that you were not born here. Your stride is not of the same length as theirs; your bearing is not quite so firm; you do not speak the language like one who learned it on his mother's knee, and the words have a different sound in your mouth. Besides, your companions all have dark skin and eyes, while your skin is light, your eyes blue, your beard a medium brown. We have seen men like you before, but none of them lived among these mountains."

"What!" I demanded, starting forward with more than a trace of excitement. "You have seen men like me before? Where? When?"

"Oh, every now and then," he stated, in matter-of-fact tones. "Yes, every now and then they come to our village."

My head had begun to spin. I took another step forward, and clutched my informer about the shoulders.

"Tell me more about them!" I gasped. "What do they come for? Who are they?"

"Who knows who they are, or what they come for?" he returned, with a shrug. "They hunt and fish; they explore the country; they like to climb the mountains. Also, they always barter for the little trinkets that we sell."

"Come, come, tell me still more! Where are they from? How do they get to your village?"

"A road, which we call the Magic Cord, runs through our town. Not an easy road to travel, but more than a trail. They say it leads to wonderful far-off lands. But that I do not know; I have never followed it far enough. That is all I can tell you."

"But you must tell me more! Come! You must! Is it hard to reach your town? Just how do you get there?"

"It is not hard at all. This trail—the one we are on—leads all the way. You cross the first range into the next valley, then skirt the southern shore of a long blue lake, then cross another range, then wind through a wooded canyon; and in the further valley, by a stream at the canyon's end, you will find our village."

I made careful mental note of these directions, and had them repeated with sundry more details.

"Once having started, you cannot lose your way," I was assured. "Just remember this: we live in the village of Marhab, and our tribe is the Marhabi."

I thanked the speaker, and we bade a friendly farewell. A few minutes later, the six strangers were no more than specks retreating along the vast rocky slopes.

But to them personally I scarcely gave another thought. Almost in a moment, my life-prospects had been transformed. I could now find my way back to my own land—yes, I could find my way if Yasma would only go with me! Enthusiastically I turned to her, told of the discovery, and asked if she would not accompany me to America. In my impetuous eagerness, I scarcely gave her a chance to reply, but went on and on, describing wildly the prospects before us, the splendors of civilized lands, the silks and velvets in which I should clothe her, the magnificent sights to be seen in countries beyond the mountains.

I think that, beneath the shock of the discovery, I was under a stupefying spell. So wrapped up was I in the great new knowledge that I scarcely noted how, while I was speaking, Yasma walked with head averted. But when, after some minutes, my enthusiasm slackened and I turned to seek her response, I met with a surprise that was like ice water in the face—I found that she was weeping!

"Yasma," I murmured, in dismay. "Yasma—what has come over you?"

Her reply was such a passionate outburst that I was thankful the others were hundreds of yards ahead.

"Oh, my beloved," she cried, while her little fists, fiercely clenched, were waved tragically in air, "you should never have married me! Never, never! It wasn't fair to you! It wasn't right! Oh, why did you make me marry you? For now see what you have done! You have locked yourself up in Sobul, and can't go back to your own land, no, you can't—never again—not unless—unless without me!"

The last words were uttered with a drooping of the head and a gesture of utmost renunciation.

"You know I would never go back without you, Yasma," I assured her.

"But you can never go with me! I must remain in Sobul—I must! I've told you so before, and I cannot—cannot be anything but what I am!"

"No one would ask you to be anything but what you are. But think, Yasma, might it not really be wiser to go away? Remember how long we have been parted even in Sobul. And would it not be better, better for both of us, if we could leave this land and be together always?"

"We could not be together always!" she denied, with finality. "And it would not be better, not better for me! I must be in Sobul each year when the birds fly south! Or I too might go the way of the birds, and never be able to fly back!"

It was an instant before I had grasped the significance of her words. "But you cannot mean that, Yasma!" I protested, with a return of my old, half-buried forebodings. "No, no, you cannot—"

"I do mean it!"—In her tones there was an unfathomable sadness, and the humility of one who bows to inexorable forces.—"I do mean it! I know that it is so! Oh, if you love me, if you care to have me with you, do not speak of this again! Do not ask me to go away from Sobul, and never, never return!"

As she uttered these words, her eyes held such pleading, such piteous pleading and sorrow and regret, that I could only take her into my arms, and promise never to distress her so again.

Yet even as I felt her arms about me and her convulsive form huddled against my breast, I could not help reflecting how strange was the prison that circumstance and my own will had built about me; and my glimpse of the doorway out had only made me realize how unyielding were the bolts and bars.

CHAPTER XXII
THE TURNING POINT APPROACHES

When the days were shortening once more toward fall and the forest leaves were showing their first tinges of yellow, I knew that I was approaching an all-important turning point. Already I had passed two autumns and two winters in Sobul, two autumns of mystery and two winters of solitude; and it seemed certain that the third year would bring some far-reaching change. I tried to tell myself that the change would be beneficent, that the enigma of Sobul would be penetrated, and that henceforth there would be no separation between Yasma and myself; but even though I doubted my own hopes and feared some undiscovered menace, I remained firm in my determination that Yasma should not leave me this year.

More than once, when summer was still in full blossom, I gave Yasma hints of my intention. But she either did not take them seriously, or pretended not to; she would brush my words aside with some attempted witticism, and did not appear to see the earnestness beneath my mild phrases. In my dread of casting some new shadow over us both, I delayed the crucial discussion as long as possible; delayed, indeed, until the hot days were over and the woods were again streaked with russet and crimson; delayed until after the Ibandru had held their annual firelight festival; delayed until the brisk winds brought promise of frost, and more than one of the tribesmen had gone on that journey which would not end until the new leaves were green. Even so, I still hesitated when the moment came to broach the subject; I realized only too well that one false move might precipitate a storm, and defeat my purpose.

The time I selected was a calm, clear evening, when twilight was settling over the village and a red blaze still lingered above the western range. Arm in arm Yasma and I had been strolling among the fields; and as we returned slowly to our cabin, a silence fell between us, and her exuberant spirits of the afternoon disappeared. Looking down at her small figure, I observed how frail she actually was, and how dependent; and I thought I noted a sorrow in her eyes, a grief that had hovered there frequently of late and that seemed the very mark of the autumn season. But the sense of her weakness, the realization of something melancholy and even pathetic about her, served only to draw me closer to her, made it seem doubly sad that she should disappear each autumn into the unknown.

And as I pondered the extraordinary fate that was hers and mine, words came to me spontaneously. "I want you to do me a favor, Yasma," I requested. "A very particular favor."

"But you know that I'll do any favor you ask," she assented, turning to me with the startled air of one interrupted amid her reveries.

"This is something out of the ordinary, Yasma. Something you may not wish to do. But I want it as badly as I've ever wanted anything in the whole world."

"What can it be that you want so badly and yet think I wouldn't give?"

"Do you promise?" I bargained, taking an unfair advantage. "Do you promise, Yasma?"

"If it's anything within my power—and will bring you happiness—of course I'll promise!"

"This will bring me the greatest happiness. When the last birds fly south, and the last of your people have gone away, I want you to stay here with me."

Yasma's response was a half-suppressed little cry—though whether of pain or astonishment I could not tell. But she averted her head, and a long silence descended. In the gathering darkness it would have been impossible to distinguish the expression of her face; but I felt intuitively what a blow she had been dealt.

Without a word we reached our cabin, and entered the dim, bare room. I busied myself lighting a candle from a wick we kept always burning in a jar of oil; then anxiously I turned to Yasma.

She was standing at the window gazing out toward the ghostly eastern peaks, her chin sagging down upon her upraised palm.

"Yasma," I murmured.

Slowly she turned to face me. "Oh, my beloved," she sighed, coming to me and placing her hands affectionately upon my shoulders, "I do not want to pain you. I do not want to pain you, as you have just pained me. But you have asked the one thing I cannot grant."

"But, Yasma, this is the only thing I really want!"

"It is more than I can give! You don't know what you ask!" she argued, as she quickly withdrew from me.

"But you promised, Yasma," I insisted, determined to press my advantage.

"I didn't even know what I was promising! Why, it just never occurred to me to think of such a thing; I imagined that had all been settled long ago. Was it right to make me promise?" she contested, stanchly.

"I don't see why not," I maintained, trying to be calm. "Certainly, it's not unjust to ask you not to desert me."

"Oh, it isn't a question of injustice!" she exclaimed, with passion. "If I were starved, would it be unjust for me to want food? If I were stifling, would it be unjust to crave air? Each year when the birds fly south my people leave Sobul, not because they wish to or plan to but because they must, just as the flower must have warmth and light!"

"But do you think you alone must have warmth and light? Do I not need them too? Must I be forsaken here all winter while you go wandering away somewhere in the sunshine? Think, Yasma, I do not absolutely ask you to stay! I would not ask you to stay in such a dreary place! But take me with you, wherever you go! That is all I want!"

"But that I can never do," she replied, falling into a weary, lifeless tone. "I cannot take you with me. It is not in your nature. You can never feel the call. You are not as the Ibandru; you would not be able to follow us, any more than you can follow the wild geese."

"Then if I cannot go, at least you can remain!"

"No Ibandru has ever remained," she objected, sadly, as though to herself. "Yulada does not wish it—and Yulada knows best."

Somehow, the very mention of that sinister figure made me suddenly and unreasonably angry.

"Come, I've heard enough of Yulada!" I flared. "More than enough! Never speak of her again!" And by the wavering candlelight I could see Yasma's face distended with horror at my blasphemy.

"May Yulada forgive you!" she muttered, and bent her head as if in prayer.

"Listen to me, Yasma!" I appealed, in rising rage. "Let's try to see with clear eyes. You said something about fairness—have you ever thought how fair you are to me? I can't go back to my own land because I wouldn't leave you; but here in your land you yourself leave me for months at a time. And I don't even know why you go or where. Would you think it fair if I were gone half the time and didn't tell you why?"

Into her flushed face had come anger that rivalled my own. Her proud eyes flashed defiance as she cried, "No, I wouldn't think it fair! And if you are tired of staying here, you can go—yes, you can just go!"

"Very well then, I will go!" I decided, on a mad impulse. "If you don't want me, I'll go at once! I'll return to my own people! The road is open—I'll not trouble you to stay here this winter!"

As though in response to a well formed plan rather than to an irrational frenzy, I began to fumble about the room for bits of clothing, for scraps of food, for my notebook and empty revolver; and made haste to bind my belongings together as if for a long journey.

For several minutes Yasma watched me in silence. Then her reaction was just what it had been when, in a similar fury, I had run from her in the woods long before. While I persisted with my preparations and the suspense became prolonged, I was startled by a half-stifled sob from my rear. And, the next instant, a passionate form thrust itself upon me tensely, almost savagely, tearing the bundle from my grasp and weaving its arms about me in a tearful outburst.

"No, no, no, you must not!" she cried, in tones of pleading and despair. "You must not go away! Stay here, and I'll do anything you want!"

"Then you'll remain all winter?" I stipulated, though by this time I was filled with such remorse and pity that I would gladly have abandoned the dispute.

"Yes, I'll remain all winter—if I can," she moaned. "But I do not know, I do not know—if Yulada will let me."

It struck me that in her manner there was the sadness of one who stands face to face with misfortune; and in her words I could catch a forewarning of events I preferred not to anticipate.

CHAPTER XXIII
THE LAST FLIGHT

As the evening twilight came earlier and the trees were burnished a deeper scarlet and gold, a strange mood came over Yasma. She was no longer her old frolicsome self; she would no longer go dancing light-heartedly among the woods and fields; she would not greet me with laughter when I returned to our cabin, nor play her little games of hide-and-seek, nor smile at me in the old winsome whimsical way. But she was as if burdened with a deep sorrow. Her eyes had the look of one who suffers but cannot say why; her actions were as mechanical as though her life-interest had forsaken her. She would sit on the cabin floor for hours at a time, staring into vacancy; she would stand with eyes fastened upon the wild birds as their successive companies went winging southward; she would gaze absently up at Yulada, or would mumble unintelligible prayers; she would go off by herself into the forest, and when she returned her cheeks would be moist.

At times, indeed, she struggled to break loose from this melancholia. For a moment the old sweet untroubled smile would come back into her eyes, and she would take my hand, and beg me not to mind her queer ways; but after a few minutes the obsession would return. Now and then she would be actually merry for a while, but I would fancy that in her very gaiety there was something strained; and more than once her jovial mood ended in tears. I could not understand her conduct; I was more deeply worried than she could have known; and often when she sat at my side, wrapped in some impenetrable revery, I would be absorbed in a bleak revery of my own, wherein Yasma would have the central place.

Yet, even at this late date, it would have been possible to avert catastrophe. Dimly I recognized that I had only to release Yasma from her promise, and she would be once more her buoyant, happy self. But I could not bring myself to the necessary point. In part I was restrained by the very urge of self-preservation, by the threat of madness if I must live alone winter after winter; in part I was held back by sheer stubbornness, the determination not to surrender the prize on which I had set my heart. And in part I was misled by my own blindness. I still felt that I had only to win this one victory, and happiness would shine for me again; that once I had weaned Yasma from her long yearly absences, neither of us would have anything more to fear.

Had my eyes only been open, I would have been warned not by Yasma's attitude alone, but by the hints of her kinsmen. Not until later did I take note of the gradually changing attitude of the villagers, and link together a multitude of signs, each slight in itself, which testified to the unspoken reproach I had aroused. But what I did observe even at the time, yet did not properly weigh or fathom, was the uneasiness and even alarm in the manner of Yasma's father and brothers. When Karem bade farewell before disappearing for the winter, he mentioned Yasma in scarcely veiled tones, bidding me not to "clip her wings"; when Barkodu bade farewell, he adjured me not to try to adapt the Ibandru to my own nature. And when Abthar came to say good-bye, it was with the manner of one who suffers a great sorrow; the grizzled face became tender and the stern eyes soft when he counselled me to take good care of his child. But he had the air of one who reluctantly bows to the inevitable, and spoke as though knowing that his words would be without effect.

I had hoped that after Abthar and Karem and the other tribesmen had gone, Yasma would recover from her despondency. But, if anything, her depression grew as the days went by. It was as though the departing ones took with them her slight remaining joy in life; with each of her kinsmen that disappeared, some new corner of her small universe crumbled away. Her eyes would now travel toward the south as if to seek there some great and glorious good hidden from her forever; and it gave me many a pang to see how she craved what was not to be. But still my purpose held firm.

Eventually there came a day when all but a few of the cabins were empty; then a day when even those few were vacant—when all except our own were deserted. The evening before had still seen two or three belated men strolling about the village; but now we were alone, utterly alone except for the screaming wild things in the woods and the unperturbed figure of Yulada above. And now at last Yasma and I were face to face with our fate.

And now the long-incipient revolt flamed forth. It was a wild, chilly day of wind and flying cloud, reminding me of that other day, a year before, when Yasma had left me. All morning she had been in a somber mood, and I had been unable to break through her silence; all afternoon she had been standing, like one in a daze, peering up at the dreary gray curtain of clouds. My remarks to her, my questions, my pleas, my soft-toned phrases of affection, were all without effect; she heard me only as one in a dream may hear murmurs from the waking world. Never before had I been so far from her; she could hardly have been more remote had she joined her kinsmen on their mysterious flight!

Late that afternoon I was busying myself in the cabin, lighting a fire and preparing some simple articles of food, for I could not let myself spend all my time brooding like Yasma. A brilliant light gleamed in her eyes; ecstasy and longing and terror and furious enthusiasm convulsed her features; she seemed a living blaze of vehemence and desire. Urgently she seized my hand, and led me unresisting into the open; then passionately pointed upward, upward to a triangle of black dots darting across the gray heavens.

"See!" she cried. "See, the birds fly south! The last birds fly south!"

I glanced skyward, but first peered at her in fright, for it occurred to me that brooding and excitement might have deranged her mind. But except for her extreme agitation, she appeared quite normal; her eyes flashed with a beautiful flame, and her old animated, fiery self had revived.

"Let me go from here!" she pleaded, almost in a transport. "Let me go, oh, let me go the way of the birds!"

I stood as if paralyzed by the force of her words; and if she had made a motion to leave, I might not have been able to detain her.

"Oh, let me go the way of the birds!" she repeated. "Do not hold me, my beloved! I want to go far from here, across the mountains, the way the birds go!"

But dread of losing her was beginning to possess me, and I made my first defense against the wild power of her appeal. "No!" I forbade. "You shall not go! You shall stay here with me!"

"No, I must go! Yulada calls! For now the last birds fly south, the last birds fly south! Oh, I must go, my beloved!"

In these words there was an intensity of longing that was almost pitiable. But my own longing was at storm pitch; and desperately I reiterated what I had just said.

"But Yulada orders me to go! I cannot resist her call! It is burning away in me like a torment!" she wailed, and raised her arms imploringly toward the gray skies, across which another band of winged travelers was careering. "Oh, I must not be late! Good-bye, my beloved!"

And she started away from me, and in a moment might have been obscured amid the shadows.

But terror of losing her filled my heart; and I darted after her, and an instant later had her in my arms.

"Yasma! You shall not go! You shall not!" I found myself crying, in a frenzy that equalled her own. And my arms clung about her, and forced the quivering form closely to me. "You must not go! You cannot! You promised to stay! I will not let you go, I will not, will not!" And what more I said I cannot now recall; but I held her to me tenaciously, distractedly, in an abandon of fear and passion; and she could not struggle free from my clasp.

And as the darkness deepened, and a red rift in the clouds like a fiery omen marked the way of the setting sun, my madness subsided, and hers subsided too; and she lay in my arms, a limp, huddled mass.

"Let it be as you wish. I will not go," she was saying, in tones wherein there seemed to be scarcely a trace of life. "I will not go. I will stay with you here—if Yulada permits."

And she buried her face against my breast, and her whole form shook and shuddered. And as I reached out a trembling hand to comfort her, there came a weird querulous calling from the deep gloom above; and I knew that still another flying thing, perhaps the last, had gone gliding on its way beyond the mountains.

CHAPTER XXIV
THE WILL OF YULADA

A gain it was winter in Sobul. The snow lay deep in the deserted fields, and in the woods it wove strange arabesques about the limbs of leafless trees; the mountains were white with vast majestic new draperies. At times the blizzards came moaning out of the northwest, with driving flakes and gales; at times the sky was icy clear and scarcely a breeze stirred amid the charmed silences. But whether the day was bright or tempest-blurred could matter little now, for all days alike were desolate in this saddest of winters.

Not long after the last birds had flown south, I began to repent of my madness in detaining Yasma. Once that fierce culminating revolt had collapsed, she did not flame forth any more in rebellion or protest; but I would have welcomed a return of the old impetuous spirit. She was gentle now, exceedingly kindly and gentle; she would hover by me fondly, and her words would be soft-spoken and affectionate; but she was no longer her old self. Something had gone out of her that had made her spirit like fire; and something with the touch of frost had taken its place. The dreary mood of the autumn, with its mute and morbid musing, had not left her even now; but with it another mood was mingled, a chilling mood, a mood as of one dazed and frightened. But of what she was frightened she would not say; she was afraid of the outdoors, and would never go forth except in my company, and then never far; and she liked best of all to linger amid the shadows of the cabin, gazing into the golden log blaze or merely staring at the blank walls and brooding.

And always she appeared to be cold, both mentally and physically cold. An abnormal apathy, almost a lethargy, had drained all her interest in life; she seemed to have few ideas except those which I suggested to her; and blue days and gray days were all as one to her. When I spoke, she would answer, but usually only in monosyllables; she would agree to every statement as though the world held nothing worth disputing; she had the manner of one whose visible form occupies this earth, but whose spirit dwells far-off.

Yet scarcely less disturbing than her mental inertia was the actual bodily cold she felt. She was always shivering, and not seldom when I took the little hands in mine I found them icy. The heavy goatskin robes, which I stripped from my own back and piled about her, seemed without effect; she still shivered, as though the very blood in her veins were chilled. And she hardly seemed to care whether or not she was cold, and, except for my little attentions, might have suffered perpetually. Reluctantly I told myself that she was leading a life for which nature had not fitted her; that she would have done better to join her tribesmen in their migration.

And there came a time when, ironically, I began to wish that she could follow her tribesmen. Alarm was springing up full-fledged in my heart, and I wondered whether her absence could be half so sad as the change that had come over her; whether it would not be far better to lose her for half the year and receive her back, buoyant and happy, along with the first spring flowers. For days I pondered, in dreadful agony of mind; and at last, seeing her growing even more melancholy and more detached, I decided to advise the very step I had once forbidden.

Shall I ever forget the time when I mentioned this most painful subject? ... forget the hurt look in her eyes, the mute reproach? It was on a December evening, when dusk had already engulfed the world, and the wind went soughing by with a distressing monotone, and the wolves on unseen mountain slopes matched the gale in the monody of their wailing. All afternoon I had been noticing how like a languishing flower Yasma looked, with her pale cheeks and drooping eyes; and terror had come upon me, the terror of things I dared not express. Even now I could not suggest Yasma's departure without the pangs of self-sacrifice; but when I saw her huddled in a corner, a pitiable figure that scarcely took note of the leaping firelight and that responded in silence to my caresses, I felt that I had no longer any choice, and hesitatingly proposed the solution that betokened my defeat.

"Yasma," said I, gently, coming to her and taking her hand, "what are you so sad about? Are you still sorry I would not let you go away?"

She turned about slowly, and looked at me with big eyes full of sorrow. "Why do you ask?" she questioned, with none of her old animation. "Why do you ask what you already know?"

"I do not know," I said, quite truthfully, "why you should be so unhappy, Yasma. But it is certain that you are unhappy, and that is all that counts. It hurts me deeply to see you so, and I think that I have been very, very wrong. I cannot adapt your nature to my own, and it was foolish to try. So I want you to forget everything I said before; I am willing for you to go away if you like, and join your kinsmen until the green leaves are once more on the trees."

For a moment she stared at me as if she did not quite comprehend. Then a wistful light came into her eyes, to smolder away in a sad glow, as of one who knows she desires in vain. But there was just a trace of the old energy in her voice as she replied, with words that burned like a rebuke, "Why do you tell me this now? Why did you not tell me before, when the red leaves were still on the trees and the birds were still flying south?"

"I should have told you before," I pleaded, abjectly. "I should have told you. Forgive me, my darling, I did not understand. But is there not time even now? Think, it will be whole long months yet before the spring breezes blow!"

"It is too late!" she sighed. "Too late! I could not go now. It is too cold. I would not know the way. The last bird has flown south. It is too late!"

In her tones there was such finality that I knew it would be futile to protest.

For minutes I stood there before her in silence, burdened with a sadness that equalled her own, face to face with a certainty I had never contemplated before. Perhaps, in that first moment of realization, I did not sufficiently conceal my forebodings, for in the end I felt a gentle hand tugging at mine, and looked down to see a wanly smiling face peering at me with pathetic kindliness and sympathy. And for a moment I enveloped Yasma's frail figure in an embrace of such fury as I had seldom bestowed.

But her form, at first rigid, quickly grew limp in my clasp; and, with renewed apprehensions, I released her.

For a few seconds she turned from me to stare into the dwindling fire; then her whole body was shaken by a spasmodic twinge, like an electric shock. And facing me again, she murmured, sorrowfully, "It is too late, my beloved, too late. But do not be sad. It is no one's fault. You could not be different if you wished, and I could not be. And one of us must suffer the cost."

"Do not say that, Yasma!" I protested, in rising alarm. "What cost can there be?"

"Yulada alone can answer," she returned, calmly but in tones of certainty. "But better that it should be I—"

"No, no!" I interrupted, furiously. "It is I that should suffer—I—"

But my sentence was never finished. Yasma had again turned aside, her whole form suddenly convulsive. It was long before I could comfort her; and late into that dismal night, while the wind clamored even more frantically without and the fire within sank untended to a smoky glow, I hovered despairingly at her side, warming the chilly hands, coaxing and caressing and pleading, murmuring reassuring words I could not feel, and all the while disconsolate because she seemed beyond the power of my consolation.

Eventually, after what may have been hours, the tumult ebbed away, and she lay impassive in my arms, like one meekly resigned when there is no longer any purpose in struggling. Her eyes had grown listless and weary; her whole frame seemed without energy; it was as though she had expended her last reserves of emotion. And in the end sleep came, impartial sleep that could never have been more welcome; and she lay huddled in my arms, unconscious of my long dreary vigil, her breath rising and falling so faintly that at times I scarcely heard it at all and listened in alarm for the feeble, reassuring beating of her heart.

But if her present state was disturbing, she was to give me double cause for concern as the days went by. Her languid and indifferent mood persisted; she showed no more passionate flashes, no more upsurgings of revolt; she had the sad submissiveness of a nun who has taken the last irrevocable vows. And, all the while, a disquieting physical change was coming over her. The color was being drained from her cheeks, which were assuming a waxen hue; the blue veins were standing out on her forehead; her face was growing drawn and thin, with a forlorn, almost ghostly beauty; her hands were seemingly without strength, and hollows began to appear about the palms and wrists. Only her vivid dark eyes remained unchanged, her dark eyes and her auburn ringlets.

I would have been less than human had I not fought with all my strength against the cruel transformation. Yet what, after all, could I do? I would spend hours in tending her simplest physical needs, in building fires, in keeping her warmly clothed, in fetching water and preparing food; but it seemed as if she were above all mere physical attentions. She would scarcely put forth an effort to safeguard herself; she would expose herself recklessly or unthinkingly to the cold; and would hardly touch the morsels I made ready for her with hopeful care. To argue with her, to coax her, to entreat her, was but a waste of time; she remained immune to the power of my persuasion and of my love; and I had the unhappy fate of watching her sinking and fading while I was unable to reach out a succoring hand.

After the days had begun to grow longer and December storms had made way for January blizzards, a still more distressing change took place. Until now Yasma had been able to go occasionally into the open, leaning upon my arm and breathing a few breaths of the refreshing breeze when the day was not too cold; but even this privilege was to be taken from her. There came a morning when, perhaps incautiously, we ventured out into the clear tingling air following a snow-storm; but we had not gone twenty paces when I felt Yasma's form sagging; and I thrust my arms about her just in time to save her from sinking into the snow. To bear the fainting girl back to the cabin and revive her was a matter of a few minutes; but she came out of this new trial weaker than ever, and was filled with such dread of the open that she would no longer leave shelter. She did not now hover brooding in a corner; she lay almost motionless on her couch of straw, covered with goatskin robes, uncomplaining, and speaking but little. And now came the real ordeal for us both. Fear, always muffled before by reason and hope, was rising unrelieved within me; I passed my days in a nightmare, tormented by my own thoughts, tortured by sight of her, and by remorse at my folly in bringing Yasma to this plight. But it was useless to waste time condemning myself, useless to let terror paralyze me. Whatever there was that I could do, that I did almost with passion; I would stir the fire into a blaze as eagerly as though the flames might fan Yasma's flagging spirits; I would prepare some poor broth of dried beans or peas as zealously as though it might put fresh strength into her drooping limbs. Yet all the while I realized that I was waging a hopeless fight. What she needed was the most skillful medical aid, the most tender nursing and carefully selected food—and how provide these here in this wilderness, alone among the crags and the snow?

But, to judge from her own state of mind, no means at the disposal of science would have been of much use. She bore the aspect of one waiting,

waiting for the imminent and the inevitable; and she seemed to feel as if by instinct that her fate was foreordained. Sometimes she would call me to her, and in feeble tones confide that she loved me, and that I should not worry; sometimes she would merely take my hand, and speak by a silence more moving than words. Of our few brief conversations there is only an occasional phrase that I can recall: how once a bright light came into her eyes, and she murmured that she had been happy, very happy with me; how one moment she would say that she was tired, and the next moment that she was cold, but always that I was very good to her; how at times her wan face would be seamed with sorrow, and she would sigh that she did not wish to leave me alone. But most distinctly of all I remember the occasion when she sat up halfway on her couch, and her countenance was transfused with a radiance that brought reminders of her old self, and she held out a pleading hand to me and whispered that I should not be sad no matter what happened; that she would not be sad, but would be marvelously happy. And in her eyes I noticed a beautiful glitter that might have been the brilliance of delirium, and might have been the exaltation of one who sees that which is hidden from most men.

Of course, I would always try to reassure her; would tell her that there was nothing to be sad about, and that all would again be as it had been. But in my heart I knew that this was not so. And my eyes showed me signs that were far from hopeful. Gradually she was growing thinner still; her cheeks, ashen before, were brightening with a hectic glow. And when I placed my hand on her forehead, I realized that she was burning with fever. Just how severe that fever was, I could not tell; but my one consolation was that she did not appear to suffer.

And now my hours were passed in continual dread. I scarcely dared leave the cabin even to obtain water from the creek a stone's throw away; I was reluctant to desert my post for brief sleep at night. Perhaps I too was growing emaciated and weak, but could that matter when my whole world was withering away before my eyes?

At last the long-protracted January days were over, and February was ushered in by the songs of a demon wind. And with February a faint hope, remote and candle-dim, came flickering into my heart, for now the return of spring and the revival of the universe seemed not quite so distant. But that hope was to be snuffed out almost at birth.

The month was still young when the shattering day arrived. The sun had come out bright and clear over the fields and slopes of snow; and toward noon a few clouds had gathered, lazy and slow-drifting and scarcely disturbing the serene blue. Responsive to the tranquility of earth and sky, my mood was more placid than for weeks; and Yasma too seemed to feel the charmed peace, for her face showed a calm as of utter content, and the fever had apparently receded and left her cheeks almost their normal rose-hue. She did not speak much, but it seemed to me that her eyes had more alertness than for many days; and when she did break silence with a whisper, it was to assure me of her love in tones unforgettably tender.

How often I was to remember those words in later days, to treasure them, to repeat them over and over to myself like some old tune whose magic never fails! But at the time I did not foresee how precious these few hours were to be. Even when evening was approaching and Yasma's eyes began to glitter as with some secret ecstasy, I did not realize that the present moment might dominate all other moments in my life; and when sunset was setting fire to the west and the stray clouds wore vermilion and purple, I was still unprepared for what the night had in store.

Dusk was falling over the world and in our cabin a lively blaze was beaming, when I was surprised to see Yasma draw herself up to a sitting posture and throw out her hands as though invoking some unseen power. In her face there was a light as of one who gazes at some ravishing beauty; she seemed utterly overmastered and borne out of herself.

"Yasma," I murmured, myself overawed at her fierce transport. "Yasma, what is it?"

She turned to me with eyes that burned and sparkled as in the first ardor of our love. Her features were transfigured and glorified; it was as though she were yearning, straining upward toward something unspeakably lovely.

"I see the birds!" she cried, with a passion she had not shown for months. "I see the wild birds! They are calling, calling! Oh, I must join them! I must go where the flowers are! I must go, my beloved, I must go!"

"What are you saying, Yasma?" I burst forth, in a frenzy of terror. "Are you out of your senses? There are no birds near us now!"

She bent upon me a gaze in which her ecstasy seemed to be crossed by a fugitive tenderness. "Yes, there are, there are! I hear them! They call to me! But do not be sorry, my beloved. I will be happier, oh, so happy! The birds are calling me—I must follow them, follow them south—only"— here she hesitated just the fraction of a second—"only, this time I shall not return!"

"Oh, do not speak so strangely, Yasma!" I pleaded, half beside myself.

But she was already beyond reach of my appeals. "I see the birds! I see the wild birds!" she repeated, rising to a crescendo of exaltation. "I will fly with them, fly south, fly south! I will go where the sun always shines! I will go where all things are green and fair! Oh, I am going, I am going!"

Once more she turned passionately toward me; but her voice faltered, and a note of something wistful and gentle softened her fervid outburst. "Good-bye, my beloved—good-bye! I am going! It is the will—the will— of Yulada!"

At mention of that dread name, all power seemingly left her. Her thin form crumpled up and slumped down upon the disordered straw; for a moment a muffled gurgling filled her throat, and then she lay motionless where the firelight cast fantastic shadows.

With the fury of one scarcely conscious what he does, I bent down and lifted the silent figure in my arms. But she hung limp and unresponsive, and the open lips gave forth no sound, and the pulse no longer fluttered.

Then when the first terror of realization came upon me and my shoulders shook and heaved and the tears flooded down, I thought that I heard a strange sound without. Even in the unutterable depths of my agony, a rhythm as of whirring wings seemed to reach me; and some will not my own took hold of me, and brought me to the cabin door, and made me fling it wide before me. Not a dozen yards above, a great bird was poised in air; and at my approach it retreated into the twilight, speeding with swift-flapping wings upward and southward; and against the last red flare of day it was dimly visible for a moment, and then became a shadow, and then less than a shadow against the spectral peaks. And the western radiance paled and faded; and the stars came out one by one in the vague solitudes, and a faint glow to the east presaged the moon-rise; and I returned to the waning firelight, and to my grief that already was merged in a flaming remembrance.

Blue skies shone above me when I paid my last tribute to the Valley of Sobul. In the white breast of the new-fallen snow, a deep brown furrow had been riven; and into this aperture, with hands that trembled and threatened to give way, I lifted the rough-hewn oaken chest that contained the sole earthly remains of her who had loved me. Very carefully I had smoothed out the flowing auburn locks; very tenderly I had sheared off a tress, which even now is with me; then, with a tearless regret bitterer than words shall ever describe, I had looked my last at that silent, tranquil face, had slipped a scented pine twig impulsively against the unmoving form, and slowly had drawn the oaken lid into place.... And now, beneath the bright beams of the sun, under the circle of the inexorable peaks, I felt my eyes flooded with a passion that at the same time brought relief; and as the first clod slipped above the casket, it seemed to me (or perhaps it was but my disordered fancy speaking) that I heard a bird singing, singing faintly a thin elfin song, a strange, trilling song such as I had heard long before when Yasma had come to me after the bleak winter....

But no bird was to be seen, although I looked for one wistfully. And no bird was to be seen, although I fancied I heard one, at that later time when I stood bent beneath my pack on the flank of a western mountain, gazing back at the solitary valley and the white-draped figure of Yulada, aloof and invincible as ever. Before me was the trail that led toward the natives I had chanced upon last summer; before me, after months of waiting, would be the open road to my own land and civilization; before me would be the beginning of a new life, and new interests that would bring consolation, and work that would bring forgetfulness; but here in this secluded vale, with its lonely woods and encompassing peaks, I had left that which not all the golden cities of the earth could ever give me back again.